"I saw the light and wanted to welcome you home."

He stared at Chrissie, looking her up and down as if she were an escaped lunatic. Or a ghost. She could feel his gaze on her, burning her.

She held up the bottle of wine. "I thought you might like something to eat, or drink."

He stepped back and opened the door wider. "Come in."

She hesitated, suddenly questioning the wisdom of coming over here. She'd let her empathy direct the action, but somehow entering his house felt like an admission of attraction. At his expectant expression, she finally stepped over the threshold. "I'm Christine Evans. I live next door." She followed him into the kitchen and watched as he found two glasses and a corkscrew.

"Ray Hughes," he said.

"It's good to meet you." She'd seen a picture of him once before, but it had not done him justice. It hadn't given a true idea of the way he filled a room with his presence.

ROMANCE

Dear Reader,

Some stories grab hold of me and refuse to let go, nagging at me like impatient children, demanding that I listen to them. This is one of those stories. From the moment Ray, Chrissie, Rita and Paul took shape in my mind I was captivated, fascinated and frustrated by the challenges of getting the book right.

Most of all, I hope this story does justice to the brave men and women who serve their country both in and out of uniform—the ones who serve, and the loved ones who wait for them. They all deserve accolades, and the happiest of endings.

This is my first Harlequin Superromance novel and I'm delighted to be a part of this wonderful line of stories. I love to hear from my readers and hope you'll let me know what you think. You can e-mail me at Cindi@CindiMyers.com, visit my Web site at www.CindiMyers.com or www.MySpace.com/CindiMyers. You can also send snail mail in care of Harlequin Enterprises Ltd., 225 Duncan Mill Road, Don Mills, ON M3B 3K9, Canada.

Happy reading!

Cindi Myers

A SOLDIER COMES HOME

Cindi Myers

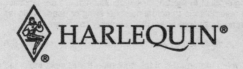

HARLEQUIN®

TORONTO • NEW YORK • LONDON
AMSTERDAM • PARIS • SYDNEY • HAMBURG
STOCKHOLM • ATHENS • TOKYO • MILAN • MADRID
PRAGUE • WARSAW • BUDAPEST • AUCKLAND

ISBN-13: 978-0-373-71498-8
ISBN-10:   0-373-71498-X

A SOLDIER COMES HOME

www.eHarlequin.com

Printed in U.S.A.

ABOUT THE AUTHOR

Having discovered at the age of eight that making up stories was more fun than doing homework or chores, Cindi Myers worked harder at realizing her dream of becoming a professional writer than she ever had at anything else. Fortunately, some dreams do come true, though she is still hoping technology catches up with her fantasies of a self-cleaning house. She lives with her husband and spoiled dogs in the mountains of Colorado.

Books by Cindi Myers

HARLEQUIN AMERICAN ROMANCE
1182–MARRIAGE ON HER MIND
1199–THE RIGHT MR. WRONG

HARLEQUIN NEXT
MY BACKWARDS LIFE
THE BIRDMAN'S DAUGHTER

HARLEQUIN SIGNATURE SELECT
LEARNING CURVES
BOOTCAMP
   "Flirting with an Old Flame"

HARLEQUIN ANTHOLOGY
A WEDDING IN PARIS
   "Picture Perfect"

This book is dedicated to soldiers
and their families.

CHAPTER ONE

HOMECOMING OUGHT TO BE as sweet as candied cherries, so the bitter regret that filled Chrissie Evans caught her by surprise. She'd expected to be past those feelings by now, to be able to join in the general jubilation over the return of another group of soldiers to Colorado Springs. She forced a smile to her lips, and a cheerfulness into her voice when she faced Allison O'Reilly, the petite blond receptionist at the dentist's office she managed.

"What are you doing here?" she asked. "You should be home getting ready to welcome that soldier of yours." Members of the Sixth Cavalry, who'd been stationed in Iraq for the past year, were coming home today.

"I've been ready for days." Allison grinned, the dimples on either side of her mouth deepening, her blue eyes shining. "The house is as clean as it can get. Once I'd put on my new dress and done my makeup, there was nothing to do but sit. I figured if I came in to work I could at least be with people until it was time to drive to the base."

"Then sit down and get to work." Rita Red Horse, the dental hygienist, patted Allison's shoulder. "You might as well take it easy while you can. That man of yours isn't likely to let you sleep for at least a week."

Allison blushed, but sat. "I'm so nervous," she said. "I can't wait to see him. And then, part of me is nervous about that, too. A year is a long time. What if he's different?"

"He'll be different," Rita said. "Paul says you can't go to war and not come back different." Her husband was a sergeant with the 10th Special Forces, on his second tour in Iraq. "But he's still your Daniel. The man you love who loves you."

"Yes," Allison said, looking reassured. "He is. And he sounds the same in his e-mails, so that's good." She shuffled folders on the desk. "Oh God, I'm so nervous!"

Smile fixed in place, Chrissie turned away and walked back into the procedure room. Only when she was alone did she allow the mask to slip, and give in to the sadness that dragged at her. She would have thought by now the grief would not be so sharp, the pain not so fresh. She'd had three years of homecomings to practice hiding her feelings, which made the intensity of her emotions now that much worse. When everyone around her was rejoicing, why was it so hard to pretend she wasn't missing out?

Trying to shake off the feelings, she began prepping for a crown Dr. Foley would install that afternoon. Keeping busy was the only way to get through this. Tomorrow would be a little better, and the day after, better still.

The door opened and Rita stuck her head into the room. "You okay?" she asked.

Chrissie nodded. "I'm okay."

"Memories are a bitch sometimes," Rita said.

Chrissie let out a shaky sigh and nodded. "Not memories, exactly. I mean, Matt never had a chance to come home."

Rita walked over and patted her shoulder. Paul had served with Chrissie's husband, Matt, and the two women had shared a bond ever since those early days when the men had shipped out for their first tour of duty together. "You want to go out later?" Rita asked. "Maybe get drunk?"

The invitation surprised a laugh from Chrissie. That had to be a good sign, that she could still laugh. "You don't drink," she said.

Rita shrugged. "I can be the driver."

Chrissie shook her head. "Thanks, but I'm okay. Just a little…melancholy, I guess."

"If you change your mind, let me know. I promise not to take pictures and use them for blackmail or anything."

Chrissie laughed again, and waved Rita out of the room. All mirth left with her friend, buffeted by memories of the only homecoming Matt Evans had had. He'd arrived in a flag-draped coffin, accompanied by an honor guard of solemn young soldiers who had avoided meeting her eyes. Twenty-five and married only eleven months—only two of those before Matt had shipped out—Chrissie had worn a black dress that was too big for her to the funeral and mutely accepted the folded flag and the medal, a Purple Heart awarded posthumously. She had been too numb and scared to feel anything.

The numbness had been a way of coping that she could appreciate now. She'd been a widow longer than she'd been a wife, Matt having been killed in the very early days of the war. Some had questioned her decision to stay in the Springs, a military town where she was surrounded by reminders of her loss. But Colorado Springs had been her home for long before she'd met and married Matt. Her parents were here. Her memories were here. The little house on Kirkham Street that she'd bought with Matt's life insurance money was here. Her job and her friends were here.

So she stayed, and she coped. She made friends with other servicemen's wives, and a few people like Rita knew her story. But mostly she didn't volunteer the fact that she was a widow. Doing so forced other women to acknowledge the same could happen to them, and that was too cruel.

On days like today, when a unit returned home or shipped out, or worse, when another funeral was held, she stayed busy and focused on other things. She took long walks, watched movies and read books. She went out with friends. She didn't read the papers or watch the news.

She dated some, but never another soldier. It was her one firm rule. Why take a chance on falling for someone else who could be killed? Why go through that particular pain again?

HOMECOMING OUGHT TO FILL a soldier with warmth—the warmth of firelight and candles. The warmth of a woman welcoming her man back into her arms.

But all Captain Ray Hughes felt now was cold, as if his chest was filling up with ice. He stood in the Special Events Center at Fort Carson, Colorado, surrounded by men and women embracing, by groups of schoolkids waving signs, by other children squealing with delight and mothers sobbing quietly with joy. He was the calm, cold center around which they all swirled.

Occasionally someone would break from their celebrating long enough to glance at him—a brief look of curiosity or pity. He looked away from them, toward the doorway, then snapped his eyes back when he realized he was looking for *her*, some small stubborn part of him hoping she'd show up, even though he had her letter in his pocket, telling him she wouldn't be here. That she'd never be there for him again.

He clamped his jaw shut, hard. There was a bad tooth on the left side. It didn't usually bother him too much, but biting down hard sent a sharp pain through his head, enough to momentarily distract him from the deeper pain that sliced through his chest as the seconds ticked by.

"Hey, Captain, do you need a ride somewhere?" Corporal Daniel O'Reilly stopped in front of him. His arm was around a young woman with blond curly hair and dimples on either side of her pink-lipsticked mouth. Dan had some of the same lipstick smeared on his cheek. His eyes had the glazed look of a man who had had too many beers, but Ray knew the corporal was drunk on the joy of finally being home after a year in Baghdad.

"No, I'm fine," Ray said automatically.

"This is my wife, Allison. Allison, this is Captain Hughes."

"Pleased to meet you, Captain," Allison said. The dimples deepened when she smiled at him.

"Is someone coming to meet you?" Dan asked. He looked around the room. The other men and their wives and girlfriends and parents and children were starting to filter out of the place now.

"I'll get a taxi," Ray said, answering—and not answering—the corporal's question.

"Let us take you wherever you need to go." Dan's wife

put a gentle hand on his arm. Her eyes were blue, her lashes heavy with too much mascara that somehow made her look even younger, like a girl playing dress-up.

To say no to her would have been too rude. Instead, he let his shoulders relax a little and nodded. "Okay. Thanks."

He collected his duffel and followed them out of the Events Center, into air so brittle with cold and dryness he half expected it to crackle with each indrawn breath. The sky looked cut from a single piece of deepest turquoise, not a cloud in sight. A blinding sun reflected off the snow heaped around them in drifts, still pristine white and soft on top.

"The snow, can you believe it?" Dan grinned at him. "Back in the summer, I used to hallucinate about days like this."

"That's April in the Rockies for you. We had a big storm yesterday," his wife said. She fished the keys to their car, a navy-blue Subaru Outback, from her purse and handed them to him. "I was worried it would delay your flight."

"Nothing was gonna keep me from getting home on time, if I had to fly the plane myself," he said.

Ray looked away while they kissed again, then climbed into the backseat of the Subaru, moving aside a plastic grocery sack full of fabric to do so.

"I'm sorry about that," Allison said, leaning back to slide the bag over even farther. "They're some clothes a coworker gave me." She smiled at her husband. "The cutest things."

"Allison is the receptionist at a dentist's office," Dan said.

He didn't know what he was supposed to say to this, so he remained silent. Dan pulled out of the parking lot. "Where to, Captain?" he asked.

Ray gave the address to the house he'd bought last year, in a neighborhood near the base.

"I turn at the light here, right?" Dan asked.

"The next light," Allison said. "They put this new one in just a couple months ago."

They'd been warned about this kind of thing in debriefing—that things would be changed from how they remembered them. It wasn't that different than if they'd been in jail. *Normal* life had gone on without them. Now they had to catch up.

Ray's jaw tightened again as they turned onto his street. Without even realizing it, he had scooted forward in the seat. He stared out the windshield, watching for the house. It was a brick ranch. A nice enough place when he'd bought it, but now it had the neglected look of an unoccupied building—the driveway unshoveled, blank windows staring out at them.

Dan pulled the car to the curb. Before he'd cut the engine, Ray grabbed his duffel and slid out of the seat. "Thanks for the ride," he said. "Have a good night."

Not waiting for an answer, not wanting to risk questions, he hustled up the walk, back straight, duffel slung over one shoulder. A man without a care in the world.

Only when he heard the car pull away did he relax and let the bag drop to the ground. He found the key where they'd always kept it, in a depression he'd chipped from a loose brick over the door.

His first surprise was that the lights came on when he

flicked the switch by the door. At least the electricity was still on. His second surprise was what the lights illuminated.

The room was bare except for a TV tray, a scarred coffee table and a recliner covered in tan corduroy. The carpet still showed the indentations where the leather sofa and entertainment center had sat. Ray stared at those small flattened squares of carpet fiber and swore under his breath. He shouldn't have been surprised. She'd picked out the sofa herself—white leather. Impractical as hell. At least she'd left the chair.

The loss of the television hurt, but he'd get another one.

He walked through the rest of the house, making note of what was missing and what she hadn't deemed worthy of taking. The air smelled of stale onions and cooking oil and pine cleanser. The kitchen looked all right. She'd left the coffeemaker, and the little table where they ate breakfast. The bigger table in the dining room was gone.

The dresser was there, but she'd taken the bed. He was glad of that. He wouldn't have to lie there now and wonder who else she'd shared that mattress with. Her clothes were gone from the closet and the dresser, though a single empty perfume bottle stood in the dust on top, as if she wanted to remind him of her. He lifted it to his nose and inhaled, and had an instant image of a laughing, dark-haired young woman looking over her shoulder at him.

He set the bottle carefully back on the dresser and walked out of the room and down the hall to the last door.

This room was unchanged. The Winnie the Pooh border she'd picked out still ringed the room. The single bed under the window filled most of the space. The rest was shared by a dresser and bookcase and plastic milk crates of toys. A fuzzy purple bear grinned at him from the bed. Looking at it made Ray's chest hurt. He closed his eyes and tried to remember what his son, Thomas James Hughes, looked like, but he couldn't.

He'd know soon enough. She'd written that she'd left the boy with his parents in Omaha. He'd spoken to his mother only yesterday and she'd confirmed that T.J. was well, but "a handful. I love him dearly, but your father and I can't wait for you to come and take him home with you," his mother had said. "We are just not prepared at our age to raise a little one again. Besides, we're supposed to leave on a cruise next week."

As if he *was* prepared. He hadn't even seen the boy in over a year. Kids changed a lot at that age.

Ray backed out of the room, then stood in the hallway, rubbing his jaw where his tooth throbbed. If he left tonight, he could be in Omaha by morning. He'd spend the night driving, instead of sitting in this house alone.

He returned to the bedroom and retrieved a spare set of keys from their hiding place beneath his socks and headed for the attached garage. The familiar smells of motor oil and old tires greeted him as he stepped into the dimly lit sanctuary. He reached behind him to flip on the light and stared at…

Nothing.

His single curse was loud, echoing off the empty concrete. He closed his eyes, then opened them again, not believing what he was seeing.

The bitch had taken his truck. The brand-new, cherry-red Nissan Titan, purchased not eighteen months ago. He'd put the title in her name, thinking he was being smart, in case anything happened to him, and she'd promised to take care of it, to drive it once a week to keep the engine lubricated, even though she said she preferred her little Honda.

She must have sold the Honda. Or maybe sold the truck.

Feeling sick to his stomach and unable to look anymore, he went back into the house, slamming the door behind him.

The refrigerator was empty, but he looked anyway, hoping for a beer. He needed a drink to dull the waves of anger and pain that kept on coming and wouldn't stop. But he'd have to call a taxi and head into town to find a bar or a liquor store and he wasn't up to that much interaction with other people yet.

So he sat in the recliner, and stared at the spot where the TV had been. He cursed himself for being an idiot, and cursed the day he'd met the woman who had done this to him, and then cursed the woman herself. Tammy. The mother of his child. The thief who had stolen his truck. The wife who had left him.

CHRISSIE ENDED UP going out after work with Rita—not to drink, but to dinner and a movie. They chose a comedy without a lot of plot, but enough laughs to take their minds off their troubles. She arrived home late and was surprised to see lights burning in the house next door.

The house had been empty for over a month now, ever since Tammy Hughes had moved across town. Though Tammy had never come out and said so, Chrissie suspected her young neighbor had moved in with the skinny private who had been a frequent visitor to the little brick house in the months preceding Tammy's departure.

Chrissie collected her mail from the box at the end of the drive, then unlocked her front door and went inside, stopping to kick off her shoes in the entryway. Her cats, Rudy and Sapphire, greeted her with pitiful yowls, tails twitching.

"Yes, I know, you're so mistreated," Chrissie said, bending to pet them, her mind still on the house next door. She hadn't thought of Tammy in a while. After Tammy's husband had shipped out to Iraq, Chrissie had tried to befriend the young woman, who had seemed so lost and alone. Despite the fact that she had a child—a little boy called T.J.—Tammy had seemed like a child herself. She thought nothing of wearing her pajamas and eating only cereal and ice cream for days at a time, letting T.J. do the same. When her Honda broke down, rather than have it fixed, she left it sitting at the curb and began driving the red truck her husband had left behind. When the city had finally towed the car—after leaving numerous citations, which Tammy ignored—she had been unconcerned. "I was tired of it anyway," she'd said.

Chrissie had gone out with Tammy a few times, giving in to the younger woman's argument that they deserved to have a little fun. They had spent one memorable evening at a bar frequented by soldiers from nearby Fort Carson. While Chrissie politely fended off the overtures of earnest young men who reminded her of Matt, Tammy drank and danced and flirted and drank some more. Chrissie had ended up pouring her into a taxi and taking her home, and got stuck with the bill for both the taxi and the babysitter.

Soon after that, the private showed up. Tammy would

call Chrissie sometimes and ask her to babysit. "I have a class at the community college and my regular girl canceled," she'd pleaded.

Chrissie suspected the only thing Tammy was studying was the private, but she'd agreed to babysit, if only for the chance to spend an evening with T.J.

The dark-haired toddler with the chocolate-brown eyes could melt Chrissie with a single gap-toothed smile. A happy child who loved to cuddle, T.J. had won Chrissie's heart the first time they'd met, when he'd taken her hand and earnestly introduced her to a purple stuffed bear. "This is Mr. Pringles," he'd said. "My daddy gave him to me."

Chrissie had never met T.J.'s father. Captain Hughes. Tammy never talked about him, except once, when Chrissie had tried to broach the subject of Tammy's frequent nights out on the town. "I'm too lonely at the house all by myself," she said, flipping her long brown hair over her shoulder, her mouth shaped into a pretty pout. "If my husband expects me to sit there all by myself until he comes home, he's crazy."

You won't know lonely until they tell you your husband is never coming home again, Chrissie thought, but she said nothing. After that, she stopped trying to give advice to Tammy. But she would babysit whenever she was asked, and spend hours rocking with T.J., reading to him and singing him songs. In those few hours, at least, she was able to fill the hole inside her where a husband and child belonged.

She carried the mail into the kitchen, the cats following, weaving figure eights around her feet. She put the kettle on for a pot of tea, and opened a can of seafood delight for the kitties. From her kitchen window she could see the kitchen in Tammy's house. The light was on, but the room was empty. Had Tammy split with her private and decided to come home?

Or had Captain Hughes returned to his empty house?

Her throat tightened at the thought. Had Tammy's husband been part of the unit that had arrived home today? How must it have been for him, standing in the crowd of joyous families, with no one to welcome him home?

The thought of that man—any man—sitting alone in that empty house after a year away brought tears to her eyes. She blinked them back and did the only thing she could think of to do. She took a bottle of wine from the rack on the counter, and assembled a plate of sandwich fixings from the refrigerator. Then she put on her coat and started next door.

She made it as far as her front porch before she turned around and went back into the house, to comb her hair and touch up her makeup. Not because she wanted to impress him, but because a man who had been away fighting deserved to look at a woman who had gone to a little trouble for his sake.

She hurried across the strip of snow-covered grass between the two houses, cold wind nipping at her ankles and tugging at her coat. She stepped carefully up the icy walk, juggling the wine bottle and the plate of food, and knocked on the front door.

She waited, the cold burning her cheeks, then knocked again, harder this time. In a few seconds, she heard heavy footsteps and the sound of a lock being turned. Then the porch light came on, and the door opened.

Her first impression of him was of strength and

height—muscles straining the shoulders of his dress uniform, his head bent to look at her. He had dark hair cut close at the sides, and dark eyes that fixed on her. "Yes?" he asked, his voice gruff.

She cleared her throat, trying to find her voice. "I—I saw the light and…and wanted to welcome you home." The words sounded stilted to her ears. Would he think she was merely nosy?

He continued to stare at her, looking her up and down as if she were an escaped lunatic. Or a ghost. She could feel his gaze on her, burning her.

She held up the bottle of wine. "I thought you might like something to eat, or drink."

He stepped back and opened the door wider. "Come in."

She hesitated, then decided she'd look even more foolish standing on the porch in the cold. She stepped over the threshold and he shut the door behind her. "Let me take those," he said, relieving her of her burdens.

"I'm Christine Evans," she said. "I live next door." She followed him into the kitchen and watched as he found two glasses and a corkscrew.

"Ray Hughes," he said.

"It's good to meet you." She'd seen a picture of him once before, one Tammy had carried in her wallet. The picture had not done him justice. It hadn't given a true idea of the way he filled a room with his presence.

He handed her a glass of wine. "Why don't you take off your coat," he said.

"It's a little chilly in here." The house was like ice.

"Sorry. I hadn't noticed." He walked into the other room. She followed and saw him turn up the thermostat.

The heat kicked on, with the burnt-dust smell of a furnace that hadn't been used in weeks.

There was no furniture in the room except a coffee table and a recliner. Chrissie stared at the chair, frowning. Tammy must have taken the other furniture when she left. Why? Hadn't she realized how cruel she was being?

But no, Tammy was not one to think of the impact of her actions.

Ray sipped the wine and studied her. "How long have you lived next door?" he asked.

"Three years," she said. Since six months after Matt had died.

"Then you must have known my wife."

"Yes, I knew Tammy." She sipped the wine and avoided looking at him. Yet she couldn't keep her gaze averted long. There was something so compelling about his face, something that drew her to study the firm line of his jaw and the jut of his nose.

At the mention of Tammy's name, his face took on a closed-off look. "Did you say your name was Christine? So people call you Chrissie?"

"Some people." She hugged one arm across her chest. Tammy had called her that.

"You were Tammy's friend," he said.

She nodded. She had tried to be Tammy's friend, but her brand of friendship was not what the young woman had wanted.

He drained the wineglass, then rolled the stem back and forth in his fingers. "She wrote me about you."

"She did?" The words—and the chill in his voice—startled her. "What did she say?"

"She said the two of you went out together. That you were single and a lot of fun." His voice was clipped, louder than it had been.

"We went out a couple of times." Despite the heater, the air in the house was colder than ever. Chrissie forced herself to stand still, to not act afraid.

Ray glared at her, a white line of muscle standing out along his jaw. "Instead of staying home with our son the way she should have, she was out running around with you. You probably introduced her to the guy she ran off with."

"No. I had nothing to do with that." She shook her head.

He hurled the glass against the wall. It shattered. She jumped, her heart racing, and set her own glass on the counter. Her hands were shaking so badly, she had to clench them into fists to keep them still.

"Get out," he said. "I don't need you screwing up my life any more than you already have."

She opened her mouth to argue, to explain she had nothing to do with Tammy's defection. But one look in his eyes told her he was in no mood to listen. She pulled her coat more tightly around her and walked past him to the door.

Once outside, she broke into a run. Only when she was safely in her own house, the door locked and bolted behind her, did she realize tears were streaming down her cheeks.

She walked to the sink and filled a glass with water, then took a long drink, waiting for her pounding heart to slow. She tried to tell herself Ray's outburst didn't mean anything. Of course he was upset; he needed someone to blame and she was handy.

But his words still stung. She'd wanted *this* man, more than any she'd met in a long time, to like her. She'd felt the pull of attraction to him the moment he opened the door and stood, towering over her yet still vulnerable. The feeling had scared her, but she'd been determined not to run from it. Not this time. After three years, she was ready to move past the hurt. To allow herself to fall in love again. The idea was as thrilling as it was frightening.

And for a few minutes there, she'd held out hope that Ray Hughes would be *the one*. The man who would help her move past the fear and hurt into something wonderful.

A man who hated her now, before he even knew her. On the scale of things, most would say it was a minor loss, but it hurt all the same. She looked out the kitchen window, toward his now darkened house. Was he sitting there in the dark, brooding? Did he regret anything he'd said?

Was there any way for the two of them to reach across the misconceptions and try again?

CHAPTER TWO

RAY TOOK A LONG SWIG of coffee and stared out the windshield of the rental car, fighting the fatigue that dragged
at him. He was still on Baghdad time, where it was
2:00 a.m. At 4:00 p.m. in Lincoln, southwest of Omaha,
the sun sat low in a gunmetal sky. He had the heater in the
car turned up full blast but he could still feel the cold radiating through the windshield glass.

He'd rented the car this morning at the Colorado
Springs airport and set out for Omaha. While he'd waited
for his turn at the counter, he'd thumbed through the phone
book and found a furniture store and asked them to deliver
a sofa, a television and a king-size bed.

"Don't you want to come down and pick something
out?" the woman on the phone had asked, incredulous.

"No. I want a brown leather sofa, a big-screen TV, and
I don't care what the bed looks like as long as the
mattress is good and not too soft." He'd given them his
credit card information, told them where to find the house
key, and they'd promised to deliver everything that afternoon.

Later, he'd find a car lot and buy a new truck. The fact
that before shipping out he had paid off the one Tammy

had stolen galled him. He'd been looking forward to having no vehicle payments.

That didn't matter now. What mattered was that he was going to get his son, and he'd bring him home to a house that didn't look like thieves had swept through it.

He gripped the steering wheel at the top and slid his hands down to rest at nine and three o'clock. Going to his parents' place always tied his stomach in knots, but never more than now. Would T.J. remember him? Would he cry for his mother?

Ray didn't want to think about Tammy, but every time he'd closed his eyes last night, she'd been there. He'd slept—or tried to sleep—in the recliner, a blanket he'd found in the closet thrown over him. But memories of his marriage played in his head like movie trailers highlighting all the best and worst scenes.

They'd met at a bar. Did single people meet anywhere else these days? The bars around Fort Carson were packed every night with men and women eyeing each other across the pool tables and dance floor.

She had been bent over a pool table when he'd walked in with a group of friends. Her dark brown hair fell like a silk shawl over her shoulders, past her waist. She'd worn a short skirt that showed off her legs, and black leather boots that ended just above her ankles. She'd glanced back and caught him staring and smiled at him, and he'd felt as if she'd landed a hook in his heart and tugged.

She'd hooked him all right. And reeled him in. He'd gone willingly, and when he'd gotten the Dear John letter he'd felt the hook rip right out. The news had hit him as hard as an enemy bullet.

She'd said she was lonely. She was tired of waiting. She was young and deserved to be out having fun. Only later had he heard from a buddy still stationed in the Springs that she'd moved in with another man.

Another soldier.

She wouldn't have done it by herself. She'd have been fine if she'd stayed home.

At first he'd been happy she'd made a new friend. Her e-mails had been full of talk of Chrissie. Me and Chrissie went out last night to a club near the base. Me and Chrissie had a girls' night out. Me and Chrissie had a lot of fun.

But Chrissie was single and Tammy was not. Seeing her friend flirt and go out with guys probably made Tammy want those things, too. She wouldn't have left him otherwise.

He leaned forward and snapped off the heater, warmed by a renewed surge of anger. Chrissie had fooled him at first, too. Last night, when he'd opened the door and seen her standing there, a bottle of wine in one hand, a plate of food in the other, a cloud of red curls framing her face, he'd thought for a moment he was hallucinating.

That she had reached out to him that way had touched him so much he could hardly speak. Watching her, feeling the wine slide down his throat and warm his stomach, he'd allowed himself a small flare of hope. Maybe his life wasn't completely in the toilet.

And then he'd realized who he was talking to and that little flame was doused.

He shifted in his seat and forced his mind away from last night, to the future. He was going to see his son again. He didn't know anything about raising a kid, but he'd figure it out. They'd do all right together. Just the two of them.

As SOON AS the office mail was delivered and parceled out, Rita retreated to the shelf in the corner she used for charting and opened the envelope addressed to her in familiar handwriting. Paul sent his letters to her here so she'd get them earlier in the day. He started that after she told him how antsy she got when she was expecting to hear from him—how she couldn't concentrate on her work, wondering if there was a letter waiting at home for her.

He'd told her his friends gave him a hard time about the letters. Why didn't he just e-mail like everyone else? But he said he thought better with a piece of paper in front of him and a pen in his hand. Even as a boy, he'd kept a journal, and his grandmother had predicted he would be a great writer. For now, his letters home were his best work.

She unfolded the two sheets of paper and smoothed them out. Paul had beautiful handwriting. His third-grade teacher was also his aunt, Wilma Blue Legs, and she had made the children practice their cursive letters in an old copperplate style no one cared much about anymore.

Rita knew because she'd been in Wilma's class, a year behind Paul. Even then she had admired the slim boy who sometimes made faces at her in the lunch room.

We have a new medic here who is from Boston. A real city boy. He found out I was Indian and he was like a little kid following me around, asking all these questions. You know the ones, all about what was life like on the reservation and all that. I told him life on the rez wasn't that different from life in Baghdad, except that here it's a lot hotter and they don't have as many tourists.

She smiled. That was Paul. He always tried to put something amusing or lighthearted in his letters. He never talked about the dangerous stuff, except in offhand ways.

You might have seen something on the news about a bombing near the base. It was a bad scene but we are all okay.

By *we* he meant his unit. His buddies. The Special Forces group who lived and worked together. *His tribe* he called them sometimes. He'd moved into Special Forces after Chrissie's husband, Matt, was killed. Paul said losing one of his buddies made him want to do something to have a bigger impact on the war. He'd thought Special Forces was the answer. She was proud of him and scared for him all at the same time, but mostly tried to keep the fear to herself, though she knew he sensed it.

I was sitting outside the barracks, watching the sunset just now. The sunsets can be pretty spectacular here. I think it's all the dust in the air that reflects all the colors. I wish you could have seen it. It reminded me of when we used to sit behind by Mom and Dad's house and watch the sun go down. I'm looking forward to doing that again with you soon. You know I love you. You're what keeps me going.

She folded the letter and held it to her chest, imagining she was holding him instead.

Chrissie passed and saw her smiling. "A letter from Paul?" she asked.

Rita laughed. "How did you know?"

"Insurance explanations of benefits don't make you smile that way."

Rita shook her head and tucked the letter into the pocket of her smock.

"How's he doing?" Chrissie asked.

"He sounds good. Of course, he wouldn't tell me anything else. He doesn't want me to worry. It's the whole stoic-warrior thing." She waved her hand. Truth be told, a sensitive, new age guy who bared all his emotions would have freaked her out. She'd been raised by people who had suffered hardship for generations. Lakota didn't emote— they endured.

She checked her watch; she didn't have another cleaning for twenty minutes. Her supplies were in order, so she had time to visit. She followed Chrissie up front, where she was pulling double duty as receptionist in Allison's absence. The little blonde had the rest of the week off to welcome her husband home.

"That was fun last night," Rita said. The movie had been silly, but silly was exactly what she needed. Seeing Allison so excited about Dan's return had brought home how many months it would be before she could expect to see Paul again.

"Yeah, it was." Chrissie glanced at her, a pensive look in her eyes. "Something strange happened after I got home, though."

"Oh? What was that?" Rita pulled up a chair and sat.

Chrissie leaned forward and slid shut the frosted glass partition that separated the reception desk from the waiting room. "You remember Tammy Hughes?" she asked. "The neighbor girl I used to babysit for sometimes?"

"The one who was cheating on her husband." Rita frowned. As far as she was concerned, there was a special place in hell for a woman who'd run around on a man while he was halfway around the world fighting in a war.

"Yeah." Chrissie sighed. "Her husband came home last night."

"He came home from Iraq?" Rita clarified.

Chrissie nodded. "I saw the light on next door and all I could think of was him sitting over there by himself. To be gone so long and then to come home to…to no one."

Rita nodded. The idea lay heavy in her stomach like a wad of uncooked dough. Paul's first homecoming, there'd been a couple of guys in his unit who didn't have anyone waiting for them at the welcome ceremony. They'd kept it together and acted all happy anyway, but everyone else tried not to look at them too hard. It hurt too much to think about that kind of loneliness.

"So what did you do?" Rita asked. Chrissie would have done something. The woman had the softest heart.

Chrissie fiddled with the appointment book, turning up one corner of the pages. "I couldn't stand thinking about him just sitting there, so I took over some food and a bottle of wine. I thought someone should welcome him home."

"Uh-huh. So what's the strange part?"

Chrissie's eyes clouded and she blinked rapidly. "It was awful. The house was cold—he hadn't even turned up the heat yet. I guess he'd been too shocked or upset to care." She swallowed and continued. "Tammy had really cleaned the place out. The only thing left in the living room was a recliner and a coffee table. The dining room was empty. No telling what else she took. It was just…sad."

"I guess he was pretty broken up, then."

"I guess…mostly he was angry. When he figured out I was the Chrissie Tammy had written to him about, he went a little crazy. He told me it was my fault for taking her out and introducing her to single men."

"He blamed you?"

"I guess…he had to blame someone. I was there." She shrugged.

"What did you do?"

"I left. I ran home and locked my door."

Rita leaned forward and put a hand on Chrissie's arm. "You don't think he'd try to hurt you, do you? Some of these guys come home and they're…well, they're a little crazy. They do crazy things." Not a month went by when the news didn't carry a story of a local man who'd hurt his wife or shot himself or someone else. Coming home intensified every emotion, good and bad, and some men, and women, too, didn't handle it well.

Chrissie shook her head. "No. I'm sure he wouldn't."

"You know to call someone if you have any doubts. Promise me."

"I promise." She turned back to her desk and checked the schedule. "Your two o'clock is late."

"Mrs. Mendoza. She's got two toddlers. Hard to get anywhere on time, I imagine. Meanwhile, you've got time to tell me about Tammy's ex. Or soon-to-be ex. What's Mr. Hughes like?"

"Captain Hughes. He's…good-looking."

Rita didn't miss the way the corners of Chrissie's mouth tried to turn up in a smile. "*How* good-looking?" she asked.

Chrissie gave up and let the smile burst forth. "Really good-looking. Tall, dark and handsome. I predict he won't be living alone for long."

"You ought to have an advantage, living right next door."

The smile vanished. "I told you, he hates me. He blames me for Tammy leaving him."

"That was just hurt talking. He'll come to his senses sooner or later. He was married to the woman. He had to know what she was like."

Chrissie looked doubtful. "I don't know about that. He was really furious. Besides, I'm not crazy about getting involved with another soldier."

"Woman, you are living in a town full of single men— ninety-nine percent of them soldiers. You are never going to find someone if you don't give one of them a chance."

"It doesn't matter. I don't think Ray Hughes is going to give *me* a chance."

A tapping on the window interrupted them.

"Sorry I'm late," Mrs. Mendoza said when Chrissie slid open the window. "Michael was fussy and took forever to get dressed." She looked back at the two little boys with her. The youngest, Michael, was about three. He rubbed his eyes and stuck out his lower lip. The older boy,

Anthony, grinned at them. Both boys' cheeks were red from the cold.

"Hello, boys." Chrissie leaned over and smiled at them.

"Hello," Anthony said. Michael sniffed and said nothing.

"I'm ready for you to come on back, Mrs. Mendoza," Rita said. She picked up the woman's chart and held open the door leading to the procedure rooms.

"All right." Mrs. Mendoza turned to her sons. "You boys behave yourselves while I'm gone."

Chrissie motioned to them. "Why don't you two come back here and play with me while your mom's getting her teeth cleaned."

When Rita and Mrs. Mendoza walked past the little office area, Chrissie had Michael on her lap and was showing him how to punch holes in colored paper with her hole punch, while Anthony stapled papers together.

Rita shook her head. If anyone was meant to be a mother, it was Chrissie. She hoped Captain Hughes would get over his temper tantrum and take a second look at the woman next door. After the rotten way Tammy had treated him, he'd be in heaven with a woman like Chrissie to care for him.

As for Chrissie, she definitely needed someone to care for. Soldier or not, Rita couldn't keep from hoping Ray fit the bill.

RAY PARKED THE CAR in the drive of his parents' townhome and started up the walk. The townhome was in one of those upscale developments that catered to older adults with money. His mom and dad had sold their house and moved here three years ago. His dad liked not having a yard to maintain and his mother enjoyed all the social activities. A year ago his dad had sold his hardware store and officially retired, at age fifty-five. Now he and Mom spent their time golfing, traveling and playing poker with friends.

At least, that's how they'd spent their time until last month, when Tammy had brought T.J. to them. From what Ray could tell from brief phone conversations and e-mails with his mom, T.J. had been seriously cramping their style.

He rang the doorbell and waited, fidgeting. After months in fatigues and uniforms, his blue jeans and sweatshirt felt both familiar and odd. The clothes were comfortable, but they weren't what his body had grown used to.

His mother opened the door and stood on tiptoe to hug him. "Welcome home, Ray. How are you doing?" She was a petite woman with short, frosted hair and smooth, unlined skin. Ray suspected she'd had a little surgical help fighting off the wrinkles, but he wouldn't have dared ask.

"I'm okay," he said. He looked past her, searching for his son.

"T.J.'s in the den with your father," his mother said.

Ray followed her into the house. "Can I get you something to drink?" she asked. "A soda or a beer?"

He shook his head. "I just want to see T.J."

"All right, dear." She led the way through the formal living room, down the stairs to the den in the finished basement. Ray heard the television and when he stepped into the room found his father on the sofa, a little boy next to him. They were watching a game show.

Charlie Hughes glanced over his shoulder when they entered, frowning. "Hello, Ray," he said, his voice even. The polite voice of a man who refused to make a fuss with his enemy in public.

Maybe *enemy* was too harsh a term, Ray thought as he walked over to stand behind the sofa. His dad didn't hate him or even wish him ill. But he had never approved of Ray's decision to join the military, and was a vocal opponent of the war. Ray had met other war protesters who nevertheless welcomed soldiers and did whatever they could to support them. But when his dad looked at Ray, he seemed to only see the government and the military his uniform represented, and not the man inside the clothes.

Ray looked at the little boy, who was staring up at him, one hand in his mouth. "Hey, T.J.," he said. "Remember me?" It hurt to breathe while he waited for an answer.

"T.J., it's your father." His mother rushed forward, not giving the boy time to answer on his own. "He's come to take you home with him."

"Daddy?" The toddler looked doubtful.

Ray came around and dropped to one knee in front of the sofa. "Hey, buddy," he said softly. "How's it going?"

T.J. took his hand out of his mouth. His brown eyes looked huge in his little face. *His mother's eyes,* Ray thought. He wanted to pick the boy up and hug him close, but told himself to take things slow. The child had had a lot of upheaval in his life lately.

He looked up at his mother instead. "Thanks for looking after him," he said. "It helped, knowing he was here with you."

His mother pressed her lips into a tight line. "I don't know what that woman was thinking," she said.

Obviously, Ray had been clueless about what was going on in his wife's mind. He'd been hurt and stunned when she'd announced she was leaving him, but when he'd learned she'd left behind their son, too, he'd realized he hadn't known her that well at all. What kind of mother walked out on her child?

"You know we never liked her," his mother said. "If only you had waited—"

He gave her a warning look, then glanced at T.J. and shook his head. He wasn't going to discuss this in front of the boy.

"Come into the kitchen and I'll fix you something to eat," she said. Without waiting for an answer, she turned and headed back upstairs.

Ray followed. He was suddenly hungry, not having eaten all day. He also knew he needed to talk to his mother, though it was a conversation he wasn't looking forward to.

He sat at the breakfast bar and watched while she prepared a meat-loaf sandwich. "How's he doing?" he asked after a moment.

"T.J.? He's upset, of course. He misses his mother, doesn't understand what's happened. Frankly, I don't either." She gave him a pointed look, one that said she expected an answer. An explanation.

"Her letter said she couldn't live this way anymore. That she wanted a divorce."

She spread mustard on a thick slice of rye bread. "She'd met someone else?"

He nodded. "I found out that part later. Another soldier." A civilian would have been bad enough, but a fellow soldier? She didn't think that guy wouldn't get sent off to Iraq or Afghanistan or East Podunk and she'd be alone again? Or was loneliness merely a cover for the real reason—that she didn't love Ray anymore?

His mother set the sandwich in front of him. "Frankly, I don't see how you're going to raise that boy by yourself. A child needs his mother."

"Obviously his mother didn't need him." He picked up the sandwich with both hands. The rich aroma of meat loaf and mustard made his stomach growl. When was the last time he'd had something this good? A year, at least. Maybe more. "He and I will do fine together," he said. "Men raise children all the time." He took a bite of the sandwich and closed his eyes, as much to savor the flavor as to avoid the doubt in her eyes.

"You are not the nurturing type," she said.

He opened his eyes and glared at her. When he'd finished chewing and swallowed, he said, "I don't hear you volunteering to help."

"And you won't hear it either," she said. "Your father and I raised you and now we're enjoying our freedom."

Freedom. A word people threw around a lot. He'd been fighting for freedom. Tammy had wanted her freedom. "I certainly wouldn't want to interfere with that," he said.

Her expression softened. "I'm happy to offer advice by telephone, and you're welcome to visit anytime. But your son is your responsibility."

"I never said he wasn't."

He ate the rest of his sandwich in silence, while she cleaned the counters and put on a pot of coffee. "You'll need to find day care for him while you're on duty at the base," she said after a while.

"I'll find out who Tammy used. And there are plenty of day-care centers in the Springs, and soldiers' wives who take care of children."

"What will you do if you have another tour of duty?"

He'd been home less than twenty-four hours, he wanted to protest. Couldn't he get used to that idea before contemplating another tour? "I'll figure out something," he said.

She took his empty plate from him. "We leave for our cruise day after tomorrow."

"I'm going back to the Springs in the morning." He slid off the stool. "Thanks for the sandwich." That was the trouble coming to visit his folks. This place wasn't his home; he always felt like an intruder here. Visits were marked by a studied politeness, and everyone involved felt better as soon as he left.

He returned to the den. The television had been switched to a news show. T.J., thumb back in his mouth, looked around when Ray entered. Ray smiled, but the boy stared back solemnly.

Charles's gaze remained firmly on the TV. A young blonde was describing an explosion in Tikrit that had killed four U.S. servicemen and two Iraqis. Ray's stomach tightened as a picture of the crumpled remains of a Bradley Fighting Vehicle flashed on the screen.

"It's a crime," his father said. "We have no business being over there."

It was an old argument, one Ray would not be drawn into. Instead, he looked at T.J. again. The boy offered a shy smile. Ray held out his hand. "Could you maybe come over here by me?" he asked.

T.J. hesitated, considering the idea, then, thumb still firmly in his mouth, slid off the sofa and walked over to Ray. Ray patted his lap and the boy climbed up and settled against his chest, as if he did this all the time.

Ray pretended to focus on the television, but all his attention was on the boy in his lap. He smelled like peanut butter and baby shampoo. The stuff Tammy used when she used to bathe him. He weighed more than Ray had expected, a good solid weight against his thighs.

Tentatively, he slipped one arm around the boy, across his chest. T.J. didn't seem to mind and, in fact, settled more firmly against him.

Ray's eyes stung and his throat ached. He stared at the television, at the blurred image of a weather map, and tried to swallow past the tightness in his throat and chest. He was bone tired, nerves rubbed raw, anger at Tammy and life in general a slow simmer in his gut, another kind of annoyance at his parents a dull throbbing in his head. He had no idea what further tortures the future had in store for him, but if his record so far proved anything, he couldn't expect much good ahead.

But all of that was overtaken by this sense of grief and happiness and...love that swamped him now. He tightened his grip on T.J. and bent his head to plant a soft kiss on the boy's silky brown hair. "It's going to be all right, son," he whispered. He would make it all right. If not for himself, then most certainly for his boy.

CHAPTER THREE

THE DRIVE FROM Omaha to Colorado Springs went well, with T.J. sleeping most of the way. From time to time, Ray glanced in the rearview mirror at the boy. T.J.'s head lolled against his car seat, and from time to time he made soft dream noises. His son. The thought of being responsible for this little life both swelled Ray's heart with pride and made his stomach tighten with fear. He could assess a dangerous situation in a war zone and direct and care for a group of soldiers in his command, but what did he know about looking after a three-year-old?

His hands tightened on the steering wheel and he forced his attention to the road. He could learn this job the way he'd learn any other. He'd use the rest of his leave to get T.J. settled, find day care and buy a new truck. And sometime soon he'd find a lawyer and talk to him about the divorce. It wasn't something he looked forward to, but it had to be done.

He pulled into the driveway of the house on Kirkham Street in the late afternoon. The snow from the storm had started to melt, bare patches of brown lawn showing through the white in places, rivulets of water running across the blacktop. With luck, they were done with snow for the year and spring could make an appearance. He leaned into the backseat and unfastened T.J.'s seat belt. "Time to wake up," he said. "We're home."

T.J. rubbed his eyes and stared sleepily up at Ray, then extended his arms in a silent plea to be lifted and carried. Ray picked him up and carried him into the house. Balancing the boy on one hip, he unlocked the front door and stepped inside.

He had halfway expected to feel the same sense of loss and loneliness that had buffeted him when he'd returned to this house the other night. But now, in the daylight with the comforting warmth and weight of his son in his arms, he felt only relief at finally being in a place he could relax, regroup and figure out the next step in his life.

"You awake enough to get down now, buddy?" he asked T.J.

"Yeah."

Once on the floor, T.J. looked around. "This isn't our couch," he said, rubbing his hand across the brown leather.

"It's a new one," Ray said. Better than the white one Tammy had picked out. "It's our couch now."

T.J. climbed up on the sofa and settled back against the cushions. "The TV's new, too," he said.

Ray admired the new television, a forty-inch LCD flat panel. Sweet. "You want to watch TV?" he asked, reaching for the remote.

T.J. shrugged. "I guess."

Ray punched the remote and flipped through the channels until he found a cartoon. "This okay?" he asked.

T.J. nodded, gaze fixed on the screen.

"Okay, you stay here while I unload the car." There

wasn't much, just T.J.'s clothes, a bag of toys and his own overnight bag.

As he unpacked the trunk, he glanced over at the house next door. It was a neat brick ranch, much like his own, with green shutters and trim. Empty planters flanked the front steps and wind chimes hung from the eaves at the end of the porch.

"That's where Chrissie lives."

The small voice startled him. He looked down and found T.J. standing beside him. "I thought I told you to stay inside," Ray said.

"I wanted to see what you were doing."

"Okay, well let's go in now. Can you carry this for me?" He offered the boy his overnight bag.

T.J. nodded and grabbed hold of the bag with both hands. Ray grinned and they started up the walk.

"That's where Chrissie lives," T.J. repeated, and stopped to point toward the house next door.

Ray's grin vanished. "How do you know Chrissie?" he asked.

"Sometimes I stay with her when Mama goes out."

According to Tammy's e-mails, Chrissie had been her partner in crime on her nights on the town. Of course, after she met her soldier boy, she'd have wanted the freedom to see him alone. Chrissie had obviously done her part to help out.

Once inside, T.J. wandered through the house while Ray put their things away. He'd left the heat on and now it was too hot inside, so he opened a couple of windows. Maybe later he'd get one of those programmable thermostats and install it. The new bed had been delivered and set up; later he'd put the sheets on. He was still fighting jet lag and looked forward to a good night's sleep.

When he returned to the living room, T.J. was on the couch again, the cartoon now a nature program showing chimpanzees climbing a tree. "Where's Mama?" T.J. asked, looking at Ray.

Ray had spent long stretches of the drive home trying to come up with an answer to this question. He sat on the sofa beside the boy and muted the television. "Your mama went away," he said, trying not to sound as grim as the words made him feel.

T.J.'s forehead wrinkled in a frown. "When is she coming back?"

Ray patted T.J.'s leg. "She's not coming back." At least, she'd expressed no intention to do so. Better for them both if she didn't. They didn't need her disrupting their lives any further. "I—I know that makes you sad," he added. "I know you miss her. I miss her, too." Maybe not what she'd become, but what she'd been—or the ideal of what she'd been. The loving wife, waiting to welcome him home. The loving mother, taking care of their son.

"I want M-Mama!" T.J.'s face crumpled and he began to sniffle, then sob.

Ray gathered his son into his lap and patted his back. "It's okay," he said. "It's going to be okay." The words were as much for himself as for the boy.

T.J.'s sobs turned to wails, his whole body shaking, the decibel level rising. Ray rose with the boy still in his arms, and began to pace. "It's okay," he said. "Stop that. You're going to make yourself sick."

The wails went on and on. He'd never heard a more

pitiful sound in his life. All the grief and fear and sadness he had ever known was condensed into those cries. As he paced and patted and murmured words of comfort that T.J. did not seem to hear, Ray felt whatever optimism he'd mustered on the drive from Omaha slipping away. He wanted to open his mouth and join right in.

CHRISSIE HEARD THE CRYING from her house—a child's pitiful wails. They went on and on and on. What was happening over there? T.J. was going to make himself sick carrying on like that. Why wasn't his father doing something to comfort him?

She paced and spoke out loud to Rudy and Sapphire, who sat at either end of the sofa and watched her, whiskers twitching, tails flicking. "I know he doesn't like me," she said. "If I go over there, he'll say I'm butting into something that's none of my business."

She snatched up the remote and turned on the television, then turned the volume up, drowning out the sounds of crying. But though she could no longer hear T.J., she knew he was hurting, and felt a corresponding pain in the pit of her stomach.

She debated leaving the house. She could go to the bookstore or the mall, do something to distract herself. But all she could think of was that sweet little boy, crying his heart out.

She couldn't stand it anymore. "I have to go over there," she told the cats, who blinked in what might have been agreement.

She grabbed her coat and marched next door, sidestepping patches of mud formed by melting snow. She punched the doorbell hard and tried to prepare herself for Ray's anger.

When he opened the door, she didn't give him time to argue or turn her away. "I could hear T.J. crying all the way over at my place," she said. "You've got to let me help."

He glanced over his shoulder and she followed his gaze. T.J. sat in the middle of a brown leather sofa, his mouth wide open, harsh sobs shaking his shoulders. "What can you do?" Ray asked, raising his voice to be heard above his son's keening.

"He knows me." As if to confirm this, T.J. opened his eyes and saw her.

"Chrissie!" he wailed, reaching his arms toward her.

She pushed past Ray and scooped the boy into her arms. "It's all right, honey," she soothed. "Chrissie's here. Tell me what's the matter."

"I want my mama!" he sobbed.

"I know you do, hon. But she's not here right now. But your daddy is here. And I'm here." His eyes were red and snot dripped from his nose. She looked around for a tissue but seeing none, carried him into the bathroom and tore off a strip of toilet paper and held it to his nose. "Blow," she commanded.

He obliged, then let her wash his face with a cool rag. "Doesn't that feel better?" she cooed.

Ray stood in the doorway, watching them. "I could have done that," he said.

Then why didn't you? she wanted to say, but didn't. The man wasn't used to dealing with small children. "You'll learn," she said.

She smiled at T.J. "Are you hungry?" she asked. "How about some supper?"

He nodded, his face still solemn and sad.

"I was going to order pizza," Ray said.

Of course he was. "Pizza is fine, but a time like this calls for comfort food." She set T.J. down long enough to remove her coat, then carried him to the kitchen, where she began searching through cabinets.

"What are you doing?" Ray asked.

"I'm going to make this boy some macaroni and cheese." She pulled out a familiar blue box and turned to him. "Do you want some?"

He stared at her with the same lost expression as his son, but his gaze was devoid of all childlike innocence. His eyes held a wariness. And beyond that was grief and exhaustion and another sharper emotion—a hard masculinity that touched the most feminine part of her, and sent a warm flush over her cheeks.

Then he blinked, breaking the spell. "Better make two boxes," he said. "I'm hungry."

She set T.J. on the floor. He had quieted, though he still sniffed from time to time. "Come on, big boy, you can help," she said. "Ray, would you drag a chair over here by the stove for T.J. to stand on?"

"Are you sure that's safe?" he asked.

"I'll be right here," she said, smiling at T.J. Then, in a softer voice, she said to Ray, "The trick is to keep him distracted. I can't guarantee no more meltdowns, but maybe this way you can shorten the duration."

He nodded and moved the chair. "Thanks."

She filled a pot with water and set it on to boil, then opened the first box of macaroni and gave T.J. the cheese packet to hold on to. "When I'm ready, you can help me put that in," she said.

He nodded, and clutched the foil packet to his chest.

"I see you have some new furniture," she said, adding salt to the water in the pot.

"Yeah, well, I didn't want him to come home to an empty house," Ray said.

"That was smart."

He leaned against the counter, close enough that one step back would have brought them into contact. "So you can admit I'm not a moron as a parent?"

"I never said you were." She stared at the pot, willing the water to boil, every part of her aware of his eyes on her. What did he see when he looked at her? Did he still think of her as his enemy? Or as the lonely woman she was? She cleared her throat. "This is a difficult situation," she said.

"Yes." He let out a breath, almost a sigh. "For everyone."

For her, too, she thought as she poured the dry macaroni into the boiling water. A person watching her might think she'd never been alone with an attractive man before. She didn't know where to look, how to act.

She settled for focusing on the little boy beside her. He stared at the macaroni spinning around in the pot. "It looks like it's swimming," he said.

"Yes, but it wouldn't be any fun for you to swim in boiling water," she said. She gave the noodles a stir. "What should we have with our macaroni?" she asked. She turned to the cabinets once more. "We have green beans. Or tomato soup."

"Soup," father and son answered in unison.

She laughed. "Not much for vegetables, are you?"

"I don't like green beans," T.J. said.

"Me neither." Ray ruffled his son's hair. The boy grinned at him, tears now forgotten.

They ate macaroni and cheese and tomato soup, with water to drink, since there was no milk. "I guess tomorrow I need to go to the grocery store," Ray said.

She opened her mouth to offer suggestions of what he should buy, then quickly shut it. Ray Hughes didn't strike her as the helpless type. He was probably perfectly capable of buying food for himself and his son.

T.J. cleaned his plate, then sat back. "Can I go watch cartoons now?" he asked.

"All right," Ray said. "For a little while."

When they were alone, Chrissie started to clear the table. Ray put out a hand to stop her. "I'll get the dishes later. You've done enough."

His hand on her bare arm was warm and firm. He kept it there longer than was really necessary, but she didn't protest. How long had it been since a man other than her father had touched her at all?

"I'd better go," she said after a moment and turned away.

"T.J. said you babysat him sometimes," he said.

She nodded. "Yes."

"When Tammy went out."

She risked looking at him then. His expression was guarded, mouth a hard line, eyes revealing little. "Yes. She told me she was taking classes at the community college, but I suspected that wasn't true." She raised her chin, daring him to disbelieve her. "No matter what you think, I didn't approve of what she was doing. I tried to talk to her about it, but she wouldn't listen."

He looked away, his posture still rigid, but he didn't protest her explanation. "She said you were single," he said after a long pause.

"Yes. I... My husband was killed in an assault on Fallujah. In the early days of the war."

All the stiffness went out of him. "I'm sorry."

"Thank you."

There was an awkward silence. She wasn't sure why she'd told him something she rarely revealed to anyone. Maybe because she wanted him to think better of her, to realize she wasn't some wild, partying jezebel who had led his wife astray.

"I really should be going." She was scared to take things too quickly—to hope for too much. If anything was going to happen between them, he'd have to make the first move. She slipped past him, into the living room. She reached for her coat, but he took it, and held it while she fit her arms into it.

"What time should I put him to bed?" he asked.

She glanced toward T.J. She could just see his profile in the light from the television screen. "He'll be tired tonight," she said. "Make it early. By eight. Give him a bath first. And read him a story."

He nodded solemnly, a man receiving instructions for an important mission. "I can handle that. And thanks." He rubbed the back of his neck. "I was ready to pull my hair out when you walked in."

"It will get easier," she said.

"I hope so."

She hurried away, almost running across the lawn to her own house. Safely inside, she leaned against the door and took a deep breath, trying to conquer the shakiness she felt. "Oh, boy," she said out loud. She wasn't sure what had happened back there, why a man who had professed to not even like her had her so shook up. He was masculine and strong, physically handsome, and his obvious desire to be a good father to T.J. touched her. He was also a soldier on active duty who could be sent back to fighting at any time, a man separated from his wife with a child to care for. A man who could so easily make her forget common sense and caution. He was everything a woman could want—and everything she absolutely didn't need.

"COME ON, sport, time for a bath." Ray picked up the remote and clicked off the television.

T.J. looked up at him. "Are *you* going to take a bath?"

The question stopped him. "Uh, I usually take a shower."

"You could take a bath with me."

After the long drive from Omaha, a hot bath might feel good at that. He shrugged. "Sure, why not?" Father-son bonding and all that.

In the bathroom, he helped T.J. undress and started the water running, then began removing his own clothes.

"Mama puts in bubbles." T.J. picked up a bottle of Mr. Bubble from the bathtub ledge.

"Bubbles?" Wasn't that kind of, well, feminine?

"Please?" T.J. gave him a winning look.

Wanting to avoid another meltdown tonight, Ray nodded. "Okay. Pour 'em in."

T.J. dumped a generous glug of bubble solution into the water and Ray finished undressing.

He lifted T.J. into the water, then lowered himself in,

at the tap end. "Can you wash yourself, or do you want me to do it?" he asked.

"I can do it." T.J. picked up the bar of soap.

"That's my big boy." Ray handed him a washcloth, then leaned back as far as he could and closed his eyes. The hot water felt good. Even the bubbles were nice, fragrant and soft.

"Why were you away so long?"

T.J.'s question brought Ray upright again. "What did your mother tell you?" he asked.

"She said you went away to fight."

He nodded. "I'm a soldier. My job is to fight our enemies." He tried to reduce the concept to something a three-year-old could understand. "The bad guys."

"Are you going to leave again?"

He could hear the fear behind the question. This was probably the kind of situation where the wrong answer put the kid in therapy for years as an adult. He shifted position, sloshing water over the side of the tub. "I don't want to," he said. "But I might have to." He wouldn't lie to the boy, though lying would certainly make things easier. He bent forward, looking T.J. in the eye. "My job is to go where I'm told to go." He put his hand on the boy's shoulder. He felt so small and slight. "But I just got home. If I have to leave, it won't be for a long time. And maybe I won't have to go at all. I hope not. Now turn your head and let me make sure your ears are clean."

T.J. ducked his head and allowed Ray to inspect his ears. The bubbles were beginning to dissipate, leaving the water cloudy. T.J. giggled. "You have a wee wee, too," he said.

Ray looked and saw the boy was pointing to his penis.

He grinned. "Yeah. And it's called a penis." Might as well give the kid the proper words for things.

"Pea-ness." T.J. tried out the word. He looked up at Ray. "Mama doesn't have one."

"No. Women are made different." He had a sudden image of Chrissie standing in the kitchen, the soft curve of her breast brushing his arm as she reached for the salt.

She'd thrown him for a loop when she'd said she was a widow. A soldier's widow. She'd said she didn't approve of what Tammy had done. Did he believe her?

She'd been so soothing and competent. Down-home. Making mac and cheese from a box seem like a gourmet meal. Her presence had calmed T.J., but it had calmed Ray, too. And made him aware of how long it had been since he'd been alone with a woman.

"Yours is getting bigger," T.J. said, his eyes wide.

Oops. "Time for bed." Ray stood and lifted T.J. onto the bath mat, then climbed out after him. He wrapped a towel around his waist, then dropped another over T.J.'s head.

"Hey!" Giggling, the boy swatted at the towel.

Ray knelt and they mock-wrestled, laughing. When T.J. was all dry, Ray turned him toward the bedroom. "Let's get some pajamas on you. What story do you want me to read?"

T.J. spread his arms wide. "I love you this much!"

Ray stared down at his son, swallowing past the sudden lump in his throat. "I love you, too, son," he said, his voice rough.

T.J. giggled again. "It's a *book*. *I Love You This Much*. It has rabbits in it."

"Oh. Yeah. A book." He pulled the towel at his waist

tighter. "Yeah, I'll read it to you." And mean the words in a way he never had before.

WHEN SHE WAS A GIRL, Rita would have laughed if anyone had told her she'd enjoy cleaning people's teeth for a living. But she did enjoy her job. Her patients were usually nice, her boss was pleasant and her coworkers were friends. Now that Allison had returned to work after a week off, things had settled into the normal routine. Rita looked forward to showing up for work each morning, plus the job helped fill the hours while she waited for Paul's return.

"Good to have you back, Allison," Rita said as she collected the file for her first patient of the day.

"It's good to be back," Allison said. "Not that I didn't love being home with Dan, but it's nice to get into a normal routine, you know?"

Rita nodded. Normal was something they all wished for.

"We've got a full schedule today," Chrissie said, leaning over Allison to check the appointment book. "Let's try not to get behind."

"Tell that to the dentist," Rita said. "I'm always on time." She nudged Chrissie with her elbow. "So what's new with you and your hunky neighbor?"

Allison swiveled her chair to face them, eyes wide. "You have a hunky neighbor?" she asked. "What did I miss while I was away?"

"Nothing," Chrissie said. "My neighbor is in the same company as Dan so he just came home. That's all."

"Oh my gosh." Allison put a hand to her mouth. "Do you mean Captain Hughes?"

Chrissie nodded. "You know him?"

"Sort of. Dan and I gave him a ride home from the reunion ceremony. I thought his house looked familiar, but I was so excited about having Dan home I didn't pay that much attention."

"Chrissie had dinner with him," Rita said.

"I made mac and cheese for him and his little boy." She glanced at Allison. "His wife walked out and the little boy was crying and I helped calm him down. I haven't heard anything from him since."

"I figured something had happened, for him not to have anyone to meet him at the reunion ceremony," Allison said. "Maybe you should go over and see how he's doing. You could say you were worried about his kid."

"No!" Chrissie protested. "Besides, technically he's still married. And I'm not interested anyway."

"Liar," Rita said as she opened the door for her patient, George Freeman.

She was finishing up the X-rays of Mr. Freeman's teeth when Chrissie poked her head around the partition. "There's a telephone call for you."

"Tell them I'll call them back."

"No, you need to come to the phone now."

Something in Chrissie's voice made Rita go still. Her heart pounded and she struggled to breathe, and her vision went fuzzy at the edges. *Oh, dear God, no!*

"Paul's all right," Chrissie said. She grabbed Rita's arm. "He's okay. He's the one on the phone."

She nodded and allowed Chrissie to lead her to the office. She picked up the phone and punched the line button. "Hello?"

"Rita, it's me, Paul."

As if she wouldn't recognize his voice. He never called except for rare special occasions and holidays. And then she could almost feel his excitement through the phone lines. Now he sounded different. Distant. "What is it?" she asked. "Is everything okay?"

"No." He coughed. "Jeremy's gone. He was killed in a firefight near Kirkut."

"Jeremy?" Rita blinked. "Your brother?" Jeremy was in the Marines. The brothers were always giving each other a hard time about which branch of the service was the best. "That's horrible."

"Yeah." He coughed again. "They're giving me leave for his funeral. Will you meet me up there?"

Up there was the Pine Ridge Indian Reservation in South Dakota, where they had both grown up. "Of course I will."

"I should be there in a couple of days. I'll e-mail when I know more. I gotta go now."

"Paul, I'm so sorry," she said. "I love you."

"I love you, too. See you soon."

She set the phone in the cradle and stared at the desktop, not really seeing. She thought of Jeremy the last time she'd seen him, at a dinner at his parents' house right before he shipped out. Paul had been home, too, and thirty-five of the young men's relatives had crowded into their parents' trailer home. The men had teased him about his short hair and the women had urged him to "Eat, eat." No one wanted to see him leave, but everyone was proud of him following in the footsteps of his ancestors, who had fought in every conflict since World War I.

There was a knock on the door. "Come in," she said automatically.

Chrissie and Allison came into the room. "Is everything all right?" Chrissie asked.

Rita nodded, then shook her head. "Paul's brother—Jeremy—he's dead. Killed in a firefight near Kirkut." The name was familiar from news reports, but she had no idea where that really was. It was just another foreign-sounding name in a list of foreign-sounding names in the papers and on television.

Chrissie hugged her and Allison squeezed her hand.

"I'll need time off to go to the funeral," Rita said, beginning to come out of the shock a little. "They gave Paul leave to come home for it."

"Of course," Chrissie said. "Let us know if there's anything else we can do."

"Thanks, but it will all be taken care of. There are groups on the reservation that will organize the funeral. It's a big ceremony. It goes on for days." She was thinking out loud now, hardly aware of their presence.

"Does Paul have other brothers and sisters?" Allison asked.

"No. Only Jeremy." She bit her lip, thinking of his mother, Donna. Jeremy was her baby. The spoiled one. She would be beside herself with grief. "I—I'd better go finish Mr. Freeman's teeth," she said.

Chrissie stopped her. "No. We'll explain what happened and ask him to reschedule. He'll understand." She patted Rita's shoulder. "You go home. Do what you need to do to get ready."

"I'll pray for you and your family," Allison said.

Rita nodded. More of the numbness was receding, replaced by the knowledge that in a few days she'd see

Paul. She felt almost guilty but not for long. She would see Paul. She would touch him, hold him, kiss him, make love to him. Yes, they would grieve. But they would also comfort each other. In the midst of such sadness was that joy.

CHAPTER FOUR

CHRISSIE'S FAMILY HOME was a two-story cedar-sided house in the shade of tall pines on the east side of Colorado Springs. Overgrown lilacs, heavy with the promise of purple blooms, crowded the driveway along one side, and patches of dirt showed through on the lawn, remnants of years of tag and touch football games played by Chrissie, her two brothers and their friends.

Chrissie couldn't help smiling as she pulled into the driveway. While she loved her little house on Kirkham Street, this was home, every part of it as familiar to her as a favorite pair of jeans. There was the big oak where her father had hung a tire swing when she was six. There was the space under the porch where she'd fashioned a secret play house. Lilacs from these very bushes had decorated the tables at her bridal shower, and that side window marked the bedroom where she'd spent the first six months after Matt's death. Though she'd been glad to move out on her own once more, it was comforting to know this sanctuary was here if she needed it.

Her mother opened the door before Chrissie was even halfway up the walk. "It's good to see you, baby," she said, enveloping her daughter in a soft hug. "Come on inside. Supper's almost ready."

"Hey, beautiful!" Her father greeted her from his recliner, which over the years had conformed perfectly to his bulky frame. A baseball game played on the television across from him.

"Hey, handsome." Chrissie completed this customary exchange, bending to hug him.

"How are you doing?" her father asked. "How's the car?"

"The car is fine. I had the oil changed last week." This, too, was a familiar exchange. Her father seemed to feel that if her car was in good shape, it was an indicator that the rest of her life was going well also.

"The house in good shape?" he asked.

"The house is fine."

He looked disappointed at this answer. "You let me know if you need me to fix anything or handle any little problems. Don't go wasting your money on repairmen."

"Thanks, Dad. I won't." She smiled and patted his hand. Her father was not one to gush sentiment. He preferred to show his love wielding a hammer or screwdriver.

She sat on the sofa and in companionable silence they watched the game. Chrissie closed her eyes and inhaled deeply the combination of scents she thought of as unique to her childhood home—pot roast, vanilla and the Shalimar perfume her mother always wore.

"Everything's ready," her mother called from the kitchen. "Chrissie, put some ice in glasses and we'll eat."

Over pot roast, mashed potatoes and broccoli, Chrissie learned about the latest goings-on at the hospital where her mother was a nurse, the retirement party for one of her father's coworkers and his most recent attempts to defeat the squirrels who constantly raided his bird feeders. "I think I've licked them this time," he said, ladling gravy over a mound of potatoes. "I've got the feeders out on wires, rigged with a pulley system. Even the Flying Wallendas couldn't get to these feeders."

Considering how many squirrels Chrissie had seen dancing along power lines, she had her doubts about the effectiveness of this effort. But she sometimes suspected her father enjoyed his battles with the squirrels too much to ever want to completely vanquish them.

"How are things at work?" her mother asked.

"Busy." Chrissie speared a broccoli floret with her fork. "We're a little shorthanded this week. Our dental hygienist is in South Dakota at a funeral. Her husband's brother was killed in Iraq."

"Oh, how awful." Her mother laid down her fork and covered her mouth with one hand, a stricken look on her face.

"Yes, it is," Chrissie agreed. She had cycled through all the familiar emotions in the days since Rita had left town: despair, anger, grief. She ached for her friend and at the same time recalled her own loss all over again. She hated that she couldn't even sympathize with a friend without being dragged back into an emotional quagmire she had hoped to escape by now. But maybe that was impossible as long as the war continued. The families of soldiers shared the experience of war in a way civilians really couldn't; through that connection, every family's loss became Chrissie's own. She was trying to figure out how to live with that reality.

They were all silent for a time, focusing on their food.

Chrissie tried to distract herself from sad thoughts by looking around the dining room, at all the familiar things here that grounded her to her life P.M.—pre Matt. An old upright piano sat across from her. She had spent hours pounding away at scales on that piano, dutifully practicing, but never really playing well. After three years, her parents had given in to her pleas to discontinue lessons, but they'd kept the piano.

On top of the piano was a row of framed photographs, including a shot of her and Matt on their wedding day— Chrissie in a white lace gown, Matt in his dress uniform. Her throat tightened at the sight of them both, looking so very young. At twenty-four, she'd thought she knew a lot about life.

Looking back, her romance with Matt had had an unreal quality. They'd met, then fallen in love quickly, their every moment together laced with the urgency of knowing that at any time he might be called upon to leave, to fight in the impending war. Chrissie had shared Matt's excitement at the prospect; he'd looked forward to testing all his training in combat and had assured her that, with all of the technological advances in warfare, the chances of him being hurt were slim.

She'd held on to that belief as a shield against the fear that always lurked on the edge of her consciousness. That giddy optimism had allowed her to say yes when he proposed, to ignore her natural aversion to risk. And when they'd said their vows in front of family and friends at the base chapel, she'd looked forward to the years ahead, certain of their bright future in a way that only a person who has never known tragedy can be.

"I've been wondering if I should take that picture down."

Her mother's words interrupted Chrissie's thoughts. She tore her gaze from the photograph and found her mother studying her, worry lines creasing her forehead. "Why would you want to do that?" Chrissie asked.

"I thought it might be too upsetting for you to look at it."

"After all this time?" She shook her head. "No. It doesn't upset me." And it wasn't as if she didn't think about Matt even without the picture.

"Still…" Her mother's voice grew brisk and she focused her attention once more on her plate. "I hope you'll marry again one day and your new husband won't want to see that picture every time the two of you visit."

Chrissie was fast losing her appetite, but she said nothing. She had an idea of what was coming and could think of nothing to head it off.

"You do want to marry again someday, don't you?" her mother asked. "To have children?"

This wasn't a new topic of conversation; only the exact words varied from encounter to encounter. "Of course I want those things," she said. A husband and children were part of the beautiful daydream of her perfect life she sometimes indulged in. But she wasn't sure how to make that dream come true.

Her mother sawed at the tender beef with a determination more appropriate for attacking shoe leather. "Have you been dating anyone?" she asked.

"Not lately."

"A beautiful girl like you, I can't believe the guys aren't lining up to take you out," her father said. "What's wrong with young men these days?"

Chrissie shifted in her chair. Usually her mother was the only one who pursued this topic. If her father felt the need to speak up, they must feel the situation was particularly desperate. "I'd like to meet someone," she said. "I just... haven't met the right person yet." A man who wasn't a soldier. Paul's brother's death had brought home with renewed clarity the hazards of falling for a man who risked his life daily.

"Maybe the thing to do is to just get out there and date a lot of men," her mother said. "You never know when you'll meet Mr. Right. He might be someone you'd never expect."

Chrissie had a sudden vision of herself enduring a series of endless coffee dates and dinners with a string of earnest but not-for-her men. Dating for her had never been the fun, carefree time so often depicted on television. It had been an ordeal to endure on the way to happily-ever-after. All she really wanted was to meet a good man, fall in love and settle down, without having to wade through a lot of Mr. Wrongs first.

The image of Ray Hughes flashed in her mind, but she pushed it away. Clearly, he wasn't interested in her, since they'd only exchanged a few courtesy nods and hellos since the night she'd made macaroni and cheese for him and T.J.

Her mother would no doubt argue that it was up to Chrissie to show her interest in Ray by inviting him to dinner, or stopping by with the pretense of inquiring about T.J. Chrissie had debated with herself about doing these things, but she hadn't yet worked up the courage to act. The more she thought, the more confused she became.

Instead of arguing the point with her parents, she

changed the subject. "The yard looks really nice," she said. "You and Dad have been working hard."

"Yes, we have." Her mother laid aside her fork, then picked it up again, and darted a glance at Chrissie's father, who was suddenly intent on tracing patterns in his mashed potatoes with a fork.

Chrissie looked from one parent to the other, confused. "What's going on?" she asked. "Why do you two look so...so guilty?"

Her mother looked at Chrissie, a too-bright smile on her lips. "Your father and I are thinking about putting the house on the market."

Chrissie blinked, sure she hadn't heard them correctly. "Sell the house? But where would you go?"

"There are some new patio homes over by Garden of the Gods," her mother said. "We toured them last weekend. They're really nice, with a lot of great amenities like a gym and walking trails."

"Someone else does all the yard work," her father said. "I wouldn't be sorry to give all that up."

"It's within walking distance of shopping and the library," her mother added. "One of the women I work with lives there and she loves it. And you should see the kitchen in this place—marble countertops, stainless steel appliances. It looks like something out of a designer magazine. Just gorgeous."

Chrissie wanted to protest that selling the house was a horrible idea, that her parents weren't the type of people who needed marble countertops or gyms. And if her dad was tired of yard work, he should hire someone to do it for him. But she choked off the words as she stared at her mother, whose eyes were bright, and cheeks flushed, like a young girl describing her first visit to Disneyland.

Her parents were really excited about this—more excited than she'd seen them in a long time. So Chrissie took a deep breath and tried to force a smile. "I'd really miss this place if you sold it," she said.

Her mother relaxed a little, but continued to study her. "I knew you wouldn't be happy with the news. You've never liked change. But this will be best for us."

Chrissie nodded. "I'm sure it will be. I'm happy for you." She would be in time, she was sure. She simply needed to get used to the idea.

"You were always a bad liar, too." Her mother smiled. "Wait until you see these patio homes. I think you'll really like them."

She nodded again, too afraid to say anything else, for fear of betraying her dismay.

The rest of the evening passed with an air of uneasiness. Chrissie found herself looking at familiar sights like the herb patch by the back steps and the crowded kitchen pantry and wondering how many more times she'd see them. By the time she kissed her parents goodbye and drove away, she was glad to leave, worn-out from the pressure of hiding her sadness from them.

Mom was right. She'd never liked change. With so many uncertainties in life she found great comfort in routine and stability. She told herself it was silly for a grown woman to be so attached to a house—a building. Her parents and her brothers had made that house a home and they were all still well and happy. She would always have her memories of the place, and photographs.

But she knew in her heart memories and pictures weren't a substitute for a physical presence. She wouldn't be able to visit the house anymore after it was sold. She wouldn't be able to go home.

On this gloomy note, she pulled into the driveway of her own house. As she got out of the car, she heard shouts and looked over to see Ray and T.J. playing ball in the backyard. T.J. had an oversize plastic bat and was waving it like a club while Ray knelt on one knee and tossed a large plastic ball toward him. When T.J. swatted at the ball and made contact, his father cheered wildly. The little boy laughed and, instead of running to the base marked by an overturned washtub, he ran straight into his father's arms. The two embraced, then rolled in the grass, mock-wrestling.

Chrissie watched them, ambushed by a longing so intense she had to hold on to the car's door handle to keep from running over to join them. She was glad father and son had bonded so well, but sad to think that T.J. would probably never again need her as he once had.

And that his father would never need her as well. She'd meant it when she'd told Rita that Ray Hughes wouldn't have to be alone for long. Any day now she expected to see another woman by his side, and eventually moving in. T.J. would have the stepmother he needed and Ray would have a woman who could stand by him the way Tammy couldn't.

And Chrissie would have kept herself safe from the pain of seeing another man off to a war from which he might not return. It was exactly what she wanted. But as she watched man and boy roll in the grass and listened to their laughter and whoops of joy, she wondered if being so cautious wasn't merely a way of trading one kind of pain for another. She knew from experience how devastating the pain of loss could be, but was the ache of loneliness really any better? Maybe it was time for her to stop waiting for love to happen, and start making it happen.

RAY HEARD A DOOR SLAM and looked up to see Chrissie's car in the driveway next door. He hadn't seen much of his neighbor since the night she'd made dinner for him and T.J. He'd even begun to wonder if she was avoiding him. Was she still mad at him for blaming her for Tammy's desertion?

Or was he full of himself to assume she gave him a second thought? Maybe one worn-around-the-edges single dad wasn't even on her radar.

"I wanna play more!" T.J. climbed on Ray's back, his arms around his father's neck. He laughed when Ray stood, carrying the little boy with him.

"Time to go in and get ready for bed," Ray said. He started to help the boy down, but T.J. clung to him.

"Carry me!" he commanded.

Ray was happy to oblige. He liked the feel of his boy on his hip, so solid and trusting. Funny how attached he felt to the little guy after only a few weeks. He could hardly bear to drop him off at day care in the morning, and no matter what kind of day he'd had, the sight of T.J. running down the hall toward him in the evening transformed his mood.

There were still problems—times when T.J. cried for his mom, or threw a tantrum because Ray didn't do something the same way Tammy had. Ray had learned to wait these out—to let his son express his rage and frustration, then set about comforting him and putting the pieces of their relationship back together.

This parenting stuff was tricky business, and a learn-as-you-go proposition. No doubt it would have been easier with a partner. Women seemed to have a knack for knowing what little kids needed, whereas while Ray could field-strip an M16 in his sleep and knew the procedure for securing the area around a land mine, he had no idea how to persuade a child to eat all his carrots or to convince him that his mother had abandoned him because something was wrong with her and not because of anything the child did.

Inside the house, they settled into the now-familiar routine of bath, pajamas and story. Ray read *I Love You This Much* for the fiftieth time, then kissed his sleepy son and turned out the light.

This was the toughest part of the evening, after T.J. went to bed and before Ray was sleepy enough to retire. He tried watching television or reading, but found it difficult to sit still. Half the time he ended up pacing the living room, fighting a whirlwind of emotions, from anger at Tammy to worry over the future to a grinding loneliness.

At the worst of times, a little voice in his head taunted him. What if this was it? What if he'd blown his one chance to establish a real relationship with a woman? What if he wasn't cut out for marriage and family and all that went with it? After all, his parents weren't exactly warm and cozy people. And maybe all the things that made him a good soldier—discipline, decisiveness and a dedication to duty—didn't translate well to personal relationships.

Frustrated by such thoughts, he'd tell the voice in his

head to shut up, pour a beer and turn on the game. But tonight he found himself staring out the window, at the house next door. A single light shone from the back. Was that Chrissie's bedroom? Was she alone over there, the way he was here?

In the weeks he'd been home, he hadn't noticed anyone else over there—no man, that is. She didn't seem to have a steady boyfriend, and she hadn't mentioned waiting for anyone who was stationed in Iraq.

He turned from the window. What difference did any of that make to him? He wasn't even divorced from Tammy yet—he had no business thinking about getting involved with anyone else, much less a woman who clearly wasn't interested in him.

The thought of the divorce made him feel even bluer. He still hadn't contacted a lawyer or done anything to get the ball rolling. What was the hurry, anyway? Tammy had to know he was home by now and in all that time she hadn't bothered contacting him or even calling to see how T.J. was doing.

All the more reason not to get involved with anyone else right now.

"Daddy!" T.J.'s voice had a plaintive quality.

Ray hurried to his son's bedroom. T.J. lay against the pillows, clutching the purple bear, Mr. Pringles. "I want a drink of water," T.J. said.

Ray fetched the water, waited while T.J. drank, then reached to switch off the light. But T.J.'s hand on his stopped him. "Will you stay with me until I fall asleep?" the boy asked.

"Sure, son." Ray pulled a chair closer to the bed and sat. "You okay?" he asked. "Did you have a bad dream?"

T.J. shook his head. He stared up at the ceiling, then said, "I miss Mama."

"I know, son." Ray stared at the ceiling, too, as if the right answers to all the questions in his life might be written there.

"Do you miss her?" T.J. asked.

"I do," Ray lied. He said it because he thought it was what T.J. needed to hear, that he wasn't the only one with his feelings. But Ray didn't really miss Tammy. He missed the idea of her—of what he hoped she would be. Now that she was gone, he felt as if blinders had been removed. When he'd married her, he'd pictured her as the ideal wife and mother, caring for him and his children, being his partner in life. Keeping the home fires burning while he was away.

Where had that idealized image come from? Tammy had been a twenty-two-year-old kid. She was a party girl without a domestic bone in her body. Putting a ring on her finger didn't change any of that. Calling someone wife didn't turn them into one.

Knowing he was partly to blame for this whole fiasco didn't help much, though. If he'd been by himself, he might have thrown things and howled out his frustration. Instead, he could only clench his jaw, which sent a shard of pain through him from his bad tooth.

"What's wrong?" T.J. sat up and looked at him, worried.

"Nothing." Ray rubbed at his jaw.

"Does something hurts?" T.J. asked.

Scary how perceptive the kid was. "My tooth hurts," Ray admitted.

"You should go to the dentist."

"Yeah. I should."

"Chrissie works for a dentist."

"She does?" He took his hand from his jaw and looked at his son.

T.J. nodded. "I've been to her office. They have this big tooth there." He held out his hands to indicate a tooth the size of a toaster. "The top comes off and inside are suckers."

"Sugar free, I hope."

T.J. frowned. "I don't know. But they tasted good. I had a grape one."

"That's good." He put his hand on T.J.'s shoulder. "Time to settle down and get to sleep."

"You should ask Chrissie about your tooth," T.J. said.

"Maybe I will." He settled back in his chair and thought about his neighbor again. Of course, the base had a full DENTAC unit which would treat him for free, but what would it hurt to pay a visit to Chrissie's boss? Maybe seeing each other on different turf would give them a new perspective.

He wanted to know more about his neighbor, that was all. It would be a good thing to be on friendly terms with a woman who could give him advice for dealing with his son, especially one who already knew T.J. Not a girlfriend or a wife, just a friend. A relationship unburdened by the preconceived notions that had gotten him into trouble in his marriage. Something simple and uncomplicated, the way love could never be.

CHAPTER FIVE

RITA STOOD between her mother and her mother-in-law on one side of the gymnasium of Little Wound High School on the Pine Ridge Indian Reservation, South Dakota. In the shadows near the ceiling she could make out the folded-up basketball hoops and banners from past championship games. How many times had she sat in the bleachers over there, cheering on her classmates? The senior prom had been held in this space, the ceiling hung with thousands of tiny lights, like stars. She and Paul had danced together, arms wrapped around one another, so close they might have been one person.

She searched the opposite side of the room for her husband and found him, standing with his father and uncles, his shortly cropped hair and crisp desert camouflage uniform contrasting with their long braids and ponytails and worn jeans. Both his uncles wore green army jackets pinned with medals. She willed Paul to look at her, but he did not, his gaze fixed on the thirty-foot-tall tepee that dominated that end of the gymnasium, and the open casket in front of it.

Jeremy Red Horse had come home to the reservation yesterday, escorted by an honor guard of marines who stood at attention now on either side of the casket. Word of their arrival had gone out over the tribal radio station and people had gathered along the road to pay their respects to the silent parade: first the three tribal elders on horseback, in full chief's regalia, then the horse-drawn wagon bearing the flag-draped coffin, marines marching behind. And finally the paint pony, its saddle empty. More than anything else, that riderless pony had brought a knot of tears to Rita's throat. She wanted to believe the words others had offered in comfort—that Jeremy had died fighting for something he believed in, that he had given his life for a higher cause, that he was following the tradition of generations of Lakota warriors, honored and revered.

But, staring at that empty saddle, all she could think was that her laughing, handsome brother-in-law would no longer joke and laugh with them. That his loss left a hole in the hearts of all his family that might never be filled.

Her gaze shifted to the tall staff set up beside the casket. The staff had a buffalo-hair crest and was lined with eagle feathers—each feather representing a member of the tribe stationed in Iraq. Photos of these soldiers were pinned to the center of the staff. Paul's photo was halfway down. Jeremy's photo was at the top.

She continued to watch Paul as he watched his brother's coffin. They had had almost no time alone in the two days since they'd arrived back in Pine Ridge—a few moments stolen here and there. He had refused to talk about Jeremy or what had happened. This hadn't surprised her, but she worried about him. The brothers had been close, more like twins than ordinary siblings. If she felt Jeremy's loss, how much more must Paul be hurting?

Someone in the drum circle began singing, a mournful chant rising up over the steady beat of the hide-covered drums. Rita tried to listen to the words, but her Lakota was rusty and, besides, the words weren't as important as the overall feeling of the song, a venting of the grief that enveloped this place like thick black smoke, choking them. Beside her, Jeremy and Paul's mother began to sob quietly.

Rita closed her eyes and reminded herself that tomorrow morning this would all be over. They'd walk behind the coffin to the burial ground, then return for a big meal. Later, there would be sweat lodges for the men and the women. Then, until he had to leave again the next morning, her husband would be hers. She would make the most of those few stolen hours, do her best to love away his grief for that brief time.

The song ended, but the drumming continued. From time to time people moved forward to pay their respects. Later there would be speeches and much later still, after most of the people had left the gym, Paul and his father and uncles and the elders of the tribe would carry Jeremy's casket into the tepee, where they would pray and chant and allow the spirits of the ancestors to commune with Jeremy's spirit.

Rita excused herself to visit the ladies' room. Afterward, instead of returning to the gym, she walked outside, craving fresh air and seeking a break from the oppressive grief. She stood near the door and stared out over the desolate landscape of the Badlands—acres of brown, rolling land pocked with gullies, the Black Hills rising in the distance. It wasn't the kind of scenery that inspired poets, but when Rita contemplated it, she felt a swelling of pride. In this forbidding country her people had made a home. They were poor, and they had plenty of problems—crime, alcoholism and diseases like diabetes and hypertension. But they also valued family and tradition. This vigil of grieving was hard, but she accepted its importance. Jeremy had lived with honor and he would be sent into the next world with honor.

"So young to die. Little more than a boy."

The softly spoken words startled her. She looked around for their source and saw two women standing in the alcove of a second door, smoking cigarettes. Their backs were to her, and she moved farther into the shadow of the door behind her, reluctant to talk to anyone right now, to accept any further expressions of sympathy.

"It's hard on his mother," the second woman said. "Having two sons over there."

"It'll be a little easier now," the first woman replied. "Paul is the only son left. The government will let him finish out his tour in the States. They don't expect the only surviving son to go back into battle."

Rita caught her breath. Was this true? Would Paul get to stay home now? He had said nothing to her about this.

"He's going anyway," the second woman said. "My man says he told them all last night. He's going back day after tomorrow, right back to Iraq."

Rita felt as if she'd swallowed lead. Paul had said nothing to her about this—probably because he knew how much it would upset her. Why would he want to go back over there, having already lost his brother to the fighting? Why not take the opportunity to escape the danger? If he couldn't do it for himself, why not do it for his parents—for her?

She returned to the gym, hoping to see some sign from Paul that would reassure her. She entered the gym just as one of Paul's great-uncles, Virgil Mankiller, took his place in front of the casket. Though over seventy, Uncle Virgil stood tall, his faded army coat heavy with campaign medals and awards, including a bronze star. He recited a prayer in Lakota, then turned to the feather-trimmed staff. Slowly, he intoned the name of each soldier there, starting at the bottom. "Jonathon Long Bow, Kimberley Brave Heart, Jason White Legs…"

The roll call sounded on, echoing in the sudden silence in the gym. "Paul Red Horse, Michael Little Bear…" Paul stood at attention, eyes fixed on his uncle. Virgil concluded the roll call. "Jeremy Red Horse." He said something in Lakota, then translated to English. "When a soldier returns from battle, we honor him, as our ancestors have always honored their warriors. Many peoples have this culture. The American flag is draped across the casket of our brother, Jeremy Red Horse, as a sign of honor. Jeremy has earned this honor from America. And he has earned another honor from his people, that of an eagle feather, the symbol of the warrior."

A young boy stepped forward carrying a folded blanket, a single eagle feather resting atop it. The Lakota had to receive special permission from the U.S. government to possess these feathers, from a protected species, for use in their ceremonies. Virgil took the feather and held it high for all to see, chanting again in Lakota. Then he turned to a second young boy, who held a small cup, and dipped the feather in the cup. "We dip this feather in blood," Virgil said. "To show that Jeremy has shed his blood in service to his country."

Tears streamed down Rita's face, but she kept her eyes open, watching Paul, staring at his head bowed in grief. Then he raised his head and his eyes met hers. She choked off a cry and rubbed her arms as a cold chill swept over her. There was a hardness in Paul's eyes she hadn't seen before, a determination and anger that seemed no part of the gentle, funny man she loved. This side of her husband was a stranger to her and the idea frightened her. She had believed this sad time would draw them closer together, that in their sadness they would comfort each other.

Now she felt only distance, and a gulf between them she didn't know how to reach across.

"THERE'S A GOOD-LOOKING MAN out front who wants to talk to you." Allison practically sang these words when she stuck her head into Chrissie's office two days after Chrissie's dinner with her parents.

Chrissie looked up from the stack of invoices she'd been reviewing. "Who is it, some salesperson?" she asked, sure the receptionist was teasing her.

"It's not a salesman." Allison's eyes danced with mirth. "I really think you ought to come up and see him."

Puzzled, Chrissie followed Allison up front. "He's in the waiting room," Allison said, and held open the door.

"Hi."

Chrissie froze and blinked at the man who stood in front of her, sure her mind was playing some kind of cruel trick. Ray Hughes seemed to fill the small waiting room with his larger-than-life presence, and he was apparently using more than his share of oxygen, too, since she suddenly had trouble breathing. "Wh-what are you doing here?" she blurted.

"I have an appointment." He pointed to his jaw. "I have a bad tooth that keeps bothering me."

Chrissie glanced at the appointment desk. Allison grinned at her. "I believe exam room four is ready for Captain Hughes," she said, then slid the glass partition shut.

Chrissie turned back to Ray. "Why didn't you see the DENTAC unit at the base for your tooth?"

Ray made a face, wrinkling his forehead and scrunching up his nose. It didn't succeed in making him any less handsome. If anything, the gesture made him look boyish, more approachable. "Don't tell anyone, but I have a phobia about dentists," he said. "Especially those military guys. They're not much into coddling."

If Chrissie hadn't been so startled by his sudden appearance in her office, she might have snorted. Captain Ray Hughes did not look like the type who needed much coddling. She turned and started toward the exam rooms. "Come with me and we'll have Dr. Foley take a look at your tooth."

As she led the way through the hallway, she was aware of him close behind her, his steps echoing on the tile floor, the spicy scent of his aftershave teasing her senses, conjuring romantic images of intimate dinners and slow dancing after midnight. If he looked and smelled this good for an ordinary dentist's appointment, what was he like on a real date?

She didn't buy his story about being afraid of dentists, and it seemed too much of a coincidence that out of all the dentists in the Springs, he'd zeroed in on her office. Obviously, he was up to something, but what? Had he come to question her further about her friendship with Tammy?

Or maybe he needed advice about T.J. and this was the most impersonal way he could think of to bring up the subject. After all, if he'd had any interest in her as a woman, he could have walked next door and asked her out.

You could ask him out. The idea had played over and over in her head for days now, but fear that he might refuse her had frozen her. Was his sudden appearance in her office today a sign she should take a chance?

"T.J. says hello," Ray said as he settled into the dentist's chair.

Chrissie's attitude softened at the mention of the little boy. "How is he doing?" she asked.

"He has good days and bad days, but no more major meltdowns," Ray said. "He's adjusting. We both are."

"I saw you playing with him the other evening," she said. "He looked happy."

"I think he is most of the time. Though it's got to be hard on him, missing his mother."

Chrissie fastened the paper napkin around his neck, her awareness of his closeness making her clumsy, so that she fumbled with the catch. A tremor fluttered through her as her fingertips accidentally brushed his neck. *Get a grip,* she silently scolded herself. She pretended to study his patient information sheet, trying to compose herself. It wasn't as if she didn't have other patients who were just as good-looking as Ray.

Though if she were honest, it wasn't only Ray's looks she was responding to, or his sexy aftershave or killer smile or bedroom eyes. It was all of the above, plus a touching vulnerability that tugged at her heart. Other people looked at him and saw a big, strong warrior, whereas she knew more than she should about his secret hurts—his anger at his wife's betrayal and his struggle to learn to be a father to his little boy. It lent a curious intimacy to their relationship that went beyond casual neighbors, though they were certainly less than friends.

"Have you heard from Tammy?" he asked, interrupting her thoughts.

She jerked her head up, not missing the bitter edge he gave to his wife's name. "No," she said. "Have you?"

He shook his head. "I would have thought she'd at least call to see how T.J. is doing." His knuckles whitened as he gripped the arm of the chair. "I remember how happy she was when T.J. was born. I never would have believed she'd just…abandon him this way."

"She was always a good mother," Chrissie said. She felt the need to defend the young woman. She didn't understand the reasons for her behavior now, but she wanted Ray to know his son had never been neglected. "She always took good care of T.J. I don't know what she's gotten into now, but she must believe he's better off with you. And maybe she hasn't called because she feels guilty."

Ray scowled. "All I know is it's hurting T.J."

Chrissie thought it was probably hurting Ray, too, though he would never admit it. "The doctor will see you in just a moment," she said, and turned to leave.

"Wait." He put his hand out and touched her arm. "Do you have to go?"

She hesitated. She had work to do, but nothing that couldn't wait. Ray smiled, a warm look that made her a little weak in the knees. "I wasn't kidding when I said I had a phobia about dentists," he said. "It would help if you'd stay and distract me."

"All right."

Dr. Foley, a stocky man with bright red hair, always entered the room as if he'd just run in from the street, a little out of breath, his face flushed. He grabbed Ray's hand and shook it vigorously. "Captain Hughes. So good to meet you. I'm Dr. Foley. What seems to be the problem?"

"I've got a molar on the bottom left side that hurts whenever I bite down." Ray indicated a spot on his jaw.

"And how long has this been bothering you?" Dr. Foley switched on the overhead lamp and scooted a rolling stool closer to the exam chair.

"A couple of months," Ray said.

"A couple of months! Why haven't you had it seen to?"

"I was in Iraq. There were other things to worry about."

"Oh, yes. Well, I suppose so."

Ray caught Chrissie's eye and winked at her. She let out a startled laugh, then moved closer as Dr. Foley reclined the chair and leaned over Ray's open mouth. He probed and prodded and made tsking noises under his breath while Ray let out the occasional grunt. Chrissie knew the moment the dentist found the bad tooth because Ray stiffened in the chair and his face went a shade whiter. She instinctively reached for his hand and squeezed it tightly.

Dr. Foley straightened and Ray closed his mouth. "It's your last molar," the dentist said. "It needs a root canal, or it needs to come out."

"Pull it," Ray said. "Today, if possible."

The dentist frowned and looked at Chrissie. "What's my schedule like?"

She let go of Ray's hand. "I think you have time for an extraction." With Rita away, they'd kept the schedule light.

"All right then." Dr. Foley glanced at Ray. "Do you want gas?"

"No. Just give me a bullet to bite on."

Dr. Foley laughed. "That's a good one. We'll compromise with novocaine. Chrissie?"

She was already drawing up the syringes of novocaine. "Here you are," she said.

Dr. Foley grinned and picked up the first syringe. "Captain, just sit back and relax. I promise you won't feel a thing."

At the sight of the needle, Ray went a shade paler, but obediently opened his mouth to accept his fate. Chrissie busied herself setting out the tools for the extraction, marveling at how she and Ray Hughes always seemed to end up in situations that might have made anyone else seem like a lesser man—but only seemed to emphasize his real strength.

That combination of vulnerability and virility stirred long-dormant feelings in her. When she'd decided she was ready to start dating again, to open herself up to the idea of a new romance, she'd pictured herself moving into this new reality gradually—a coffee date here, a movie there, keeping things casual. She'd never anticipated the heat of attraction and intensity of emotion that almost overwhelmed her whenever she was near Ray.

She wasn't sure how to handle the onslaught, afraid she'd come across as some sex-starved widow or lonely loser. There ought to be a way to slow the pace and avoid risking so much of her self-esteem. She didn't want her first foray into a relationship to end badly. If only she could have started with some nice man who didn't stir her emotions so much, sort of like a practice relationship, before she got into the real thing.

Then again, she couldn't imagine any man holding her interest now that she'd been exposed to Ray. Whether he realized it or not, he'd already captivated her. The trick now was to explore their feelings for each other without letting him know how much he had the power to hurt her.

RITA FINALLY HAD the chance to be alone with Paul the next evening. Jeremy had been interred that morning. Then had come the rounds of visiting, the sweat lodges and a huge dinner at his parents' house, at which all the relatives gathered. Finally, she was able to pull him away from the crowd, into the back bedroom he and Jeremy had shared as children, where the two of them were staying now.

"How are you holding up?" she asked, brushing his shoulder.

He shrugged off her hand. "I'm okay."

"Hey, don't push me away," she said. "I care about you."

He looked sheepish, and took her hand in his. "I know, just...don't fuss, okay? I've had enough of that from the aunties."

"All right. I won't fuss." She stood on tiptoe and kissed him, a light brush of her lips across his, which he immediately deepened, pulling her tight against him and prolonging the embrace until she was breathless. She'd spent months now missing him and forcing herself not to dwell on that particular ache, but now that she was back in his arms, her body proved it had not forgotten how much it needed him.

He smoothed his hand down her side and rested his forehead against hers, smiling. "I've missed you so much," he whispered.

"I've missed you, too." She slid her hands beneath his shirt, working her way up his chest, reveling in the feel of his smooth skin against her palms, at the steady pounding of his heart beneath her fingers.

He took hold of the tails of his shirt and pulled it off over his head, then divested her of her own top and skirt. They moved together, in an intimate dance whose steps they knew well, every gesture accented by a tender urgency.

He backed her up until her thighs touched the edge of the bed, then they fell together on the mattress, Rita giggling as it squeaked beneath them. "Everyone's going to know what we're doing," she whispered.

"Anybody with half a brain would figure it out anyway," he said. He laid a line of kisses down her shoulder blade. "Nights when I can't sleep, I think about you," he said. "How beautiful you look naked. How amazing you feel." He slipped his hand between her legs and cupped her sex.

She was suddenly desperate to feel him inside her, to reassure herself once again that he was hers, that the distance she'd imagined earlier in the gym was only a delusion born of grief and stress and worry.

She scooted back against the pillows and beckoned him near. "Come up here and love me," she said. "Love me the way you wanted to all those nights when we were apart."

He growled low in his throat, a sound that sent a

shiver of arousal through her. Then he levered himself over her, kissing her mouth, her cheeks, her neck, lingering at her breasts until she whimpered and writhed beneath him, arching to him, whispering that she wanted him inside her, now.

She let out a moan as he filled her, months of an emptiness that had been more than physical ending. As he began to move over her she gripped his shoulders, reveling in the hard curve of muscle, marveling at his strength, and how it was possible to love and admire one man so much.

He came quickly, and she struggled to hide her disappointment, but she needn't have worried. "I'm going to take care of you, baby," he said, reaching down to caress her, his eyes locked to hers in a look so full of love and passion she felt the hot sting of sudden tears.

But as he continued to stroke and fondle, she let her eyes drift closed and surrendered to the bliss of his touch. He held her close and kissed her cheek and her neck, murmuring endearments, every feather touch of his lips bringing her nearer to her own release.

She bit her finger to keep from crying out as she came, but he pulled her hand away and covered her mouth with his own, muffling her cries with his kiss. She hugged him tightly, and blinked back more tears. "I love you," she murmured, over and over. "I love you, I love you, I love you."

They lay unspeaking for a long time, until her arm went to sleep and she had to move. He rolled over beside her and stretched his arms over his head, looking up at the ceiling. "I'm glad I got to see you," he said. "I'm glad we didn't have to wait until this fall or whenever Uncle Sam lets me come home."

"Me, too." She snuggled against him, resting her head on his chest. "Though I'm sad it had to be for this reason."

"Yeah." He idly stroked her hair, winding the strands around his fingers.

She took a deep breath, afraid what she had to say next would spoil the mood. But she had to say it. She wouldn't sleep until she knew the truth, one way or another. "I heard a couple of women talking yesterday, when I took a break for a few minutes and stepped outside," she said. "They said that since you're your parents' only surviving son, you don't necessarily have to go back to the fighting. That you could finish out your tour in the United States."

He stiffened beside her. "Sometimes that happens," he said. "But I didn't want to do that."

She swallowed hard. "Why not?"

"I didn't think it would be right," he said. "To leave my guys over there without me."

His guys. The Special Forces team. "I'm sure they'd understand," she said. "Any of them would probably take advantage of the chance, if they had it."

"My brother didn't die so I could take it easy State-side," he said.

"And I think he'd be glad his death at least gave you the chance to stay safe."

He rose abruptly, so that she slid off his chest. He sat on the edge of the bed, his back to her. "I knew you wouldn't understand," he said. "That's why I didn't tell you before."

"Then make me understand." She leaned toward him. "What over there is worth dying for? What is worth putting your parents—putting me—through the agony of possibly losing you? Isn't losing Jeremy enough?"

"Look, I don't want to talk about this anymore," he said. "I've got a job to do over there and I'm going to do it. Don't think you can pull some guilt trip on me and make me change my mind."

"I'm not *pulling a guilt trip*." She bunched the bedspread in her hands, wishing it were possible to shake some sense into him. "I'm asking a legitimate question. Why is going back to Iraq more important to you than your family?"

He stood and reached for his pants and pulled them on. "I'm going out," he said.

She sat up. "You can't leave. We haven't finished discussing this."

"I've said all I'm going to say." He pulled his shirt over his head and slid his feet into a pair of flip-flops. "Don't wait up. I'll probably be late."

Then he was gone. She stared at the closed door. Only the crowd of relatives gathered in the rooms on the other side kept her from dressing and running after him. That, and the knowledge that pleading with him now would do no good. Before, she'd always admired her husband's steadfastness, his ability to make up his mind about a course of action and stick to it. Such determination had allowed him to accomplish a lot in his young life and had earned him the respect of almost everyone who knew him.

But the other side of that coin was a stubborn bullheadedness that made him impossible to sway, even in the rare times, as now, when he was so completely in the wrong.

CHAPTER SIX

RAY HADN'T BEEN LYING to Chrissie when he told her he had a phobia about dentists. On his list of things he'd prefer to do, having a tooth pulled rested somewhere below cleaning out a septic tank and only slightly above patrolling for land mines.

So having her there beside him while Dr. Foley extracted the decayed molar was a welcome distraction. Her hand on his arm soothed him, and all the while the doctor drilled and tugged and rinsed and packed, Ray was aware of silken fingertips resting gently against his skin, reminding him of other sensations far removed from this dental chair or his everyday life: caring caresses, heated looks and intimacies he sorely missed.

He wondered what Chrissie would think if she knew the paths his thoughts took. Would she be shocked or amused to know that her gesture of comfort had him fantasizing about other ways in which she might touch him?

The idea made him smile as he sat up in the chair at the end of the procedure, though he knew his expression was lopsided.

"How do you feel?" Chrissie asked.

"Like a chipmunk," he said, talking carefully around the

wad of cotton packing in his cheek. He gingerly rubbed his numb jaw. "How long before this wears off?"

"You'll be fine in a couple of hours," she said. "Don't try to eat or talk too much until then. Be careful not to bite your tongue."

"Thanks for staying with me through the procedure," he said.

She looked as if she was trying not to laugh, maybe because he sounded like Porky Pig. "You were very brave," she said. "Would you like a lollipop or a sticker?"

He could think of sweeter things she might offer him. "How about dinner instead?"

Her eyes widened in surprise. "Dinner?"

"Sure. I owe you for the meal you fixed for me and T.J. And I'm sorry I acted like such a jerk the first night we met. Let me make it up to you."

She busied herself straightening the papers in his file. "And what's the equivalent of boxed macaroni and cheese and canned tomato soup?" she asked, not looking at him. "A fast-food burger?"

"I'd even spring for a real meal," he said. "I know a nice Italian place."

She looked at him again, all teasing vanished from her manner. "All right," she said. "I'd really like that."

"I'll meet you back at the house after I pick up T.J. from day care," he said. "Does about six o'clock sound okay?"

Her smile made him catch his breath, it was so full of joy. "I'll be looking forward to it."

Mesmerized by that smile, he didn't remember walking out to his truck or turning the key. He took a deep breath, and gripped the steering wheel tightly, steadying himself.

Take it easy, he told himself. Chrissie was a nice woman, beautiful and sweet and sexy. But no sense making a mistake on the rebound. They'd have a friendly dinner with T.J. and take it from there. No need to rush into anything.

After all, technically, he was still married. He hadn't seen Tammy in over a year and he certainly didn't feel married, but legally he was. He'd put off contacting a lawyer about a divorce because he'd been busy with T.J. and settling back into life in the States, but maybe it was time to do that. To move on and free himself up for a new relationship.

He drove to the day-care center near the base in his new truck. It was a plainer, less-expensive model than the one he'd had before, but for reasons other than that it would never mean as much to him as the one he'd lost. That had been a special purchase, his first brand-new vehicle, something he'd bought a short time before he shipped out in order to have it to look forward to when he returned to the States. Finding both it and his marriage gone had made him question why he'd bothered coming home at all.

Thank God for T.J. His son was definitely worth returning to. He'd always loved the boy, but when he'd shipped out, he'd left behind a baby, an infant who'd seemed more Tammy's than his own.

He'd come home to a boy, who walked and talked and had his own ideas and opinions. When Ray looked at T.J. now, he recognized a little part of himself, and the knowledge made his heart feel too big for his chest sometimes.

At the day care, T.J. was waiting for him. As always, he raced down the hall and threw his arms around Ray's legs, and laughed with delight as Ray scooped him up. "How's my boy?" he asked.

"Okay." T.J. patted Ray's cheek. "What's wrong with your mouth? Why are you talking funny?"

Ray reached into his mouth and extracted the wad of gauze. He was still numb, but not as much as he had been. "I had a tooth pulled," he said. "I'm okay now."

"Why did you have your tooth pulled?" T.J. asked.

Ray set him down and side by side they walked out to the truck. "I had it pulled because it was hurting me."

"Why was it hurting you?"

"Because it had a cavity—a rotten place."

"Why did it get a rotten place?"

Ray had discovered one of his jobs as a parent was to try to answer T.J.'s seemingly endless store of questions. "I was a bad boy and didn't brush my teeth the way I should," he said, helping his son into the truck's backseat. "You should learn from my mistakes." He buckled T.J. into his booster seat. "Now tell me what you did today."

All the way home T.J. chattered about what he ate for a snack, the games he learned on the playground and the modeling clay he worked with during craft time. "Oh, and we learned a new song." Not waiting for comment, he burst into a loud, off-key rendition of "Little Bunny Foo Foo."

Ray laughed and applauded. "That was great." He smiled at his son in the rearview mirror. It amazed him how he could be so happy and so sad at the same time—happy that he had this chance to know his son, who was an amazing boy, and sad because the loneliness overwhelmed him sometimes, to the point where he could have broken down and wept, though he never allowed himself to go that far.

All those months in Iraq, he'd held on to the dream of

coming home to his family. He'd savored the thought of having someone to talk to in the evening about something other than the war. Someone to welcome him to bed at night, to hold him when the bad memories crowded in, and to give him better memories to replace them.

Life hadn't turned out that way, and he was doing his best to adjust, but too often his time here didn't seem that different from his time in Iraq, fighting tedium and fear and an enemy he couldn't always see or understand—though in this case, his enemy wasn't foreign terrorists or guerilla fighters, but his own loneliness and self-doubt.

At home he parked in the driveway and retrieved his mail from the box at the street. As he walked back toward the house, he flipped through the collection of bills and junk mail, stopping at a thick white envelope embossed with the name of a legal firm. Frowning, he ripped open the envelope and pulled out a sheaf of papers. He skimmed the top page, words jumping out at him: Raymond B. Hughes…Tamara J. Hughes…*Divorce*.

He felt cold despite the bright sunlight. So Tammy had finally decided to get in touch. Not to see how he was doing, or to ask about her son, or to try to explain her actions. Instead, she was suing for divorce.

He'd known it was coming, of course. But seeing that word—*divorce*—in black and white legalese, made it hard to breathe. It was like having the word *failure* stamped across his chest. He'd failed at the one thing he'd wanted most—a good marriage. Now he was another statistic, another man with one strike against him in the relationship column.

He had plenty of company but the point was he'd never pictured himself in those ranks. Yet here he was.

He was still standing halfway between the street and his front door, trying to absorb the news, when a car pulled into the driveway next door and Chrissie got out.

"Hello, Ray," she called. "How's the tooth?"

The tooth? He'd forgotten all about the tooth. His jaw was less numb and he probably would have been able to talk if he could have found his voice. He settled for nodding. The tooth was fine. The rest of him was a mess, however.

Chrissie walked over to him. "Are you okay?" she asked. "You look a little pale."

He folded the letter from the lawyer and shoved it back into the envelope before she could see it. "I'll be okay," he said. "Just...some paperwork to deal with."

He focused his attention on her. "Are you ready for dinner?" he asked. "This place I know makes killer meatballs. It's a little out of the way, so you won't have to worry about your reputation, being seen with me." He gave her an exaggerated leer, which made her laugh, as he'd hoped it would.

"I'm not worried about my reputation," she said, her voice husky. He fought the desire to pull her close and kiss her, his resistance made all the more difficult because her eyes seemed to be telegraphing that was exactly what she wanted.

She was the first to look away, her cheeks flushed a becoming pink, her voice slightly breathy. "Just let me go in and feed my cats."

"Sure." He cleared his throat. "I'll meet you back here in, say, twenty minutes?"

"That sounds good." That smile again, rocking him back on his feet.

He was still reeling from Tammy's demand for a divorce, but now he had an excuse to put off thinking about it for a few more hours. He'd focus on a nice meal with a nice woman and forget about the future for a little while longer.

CHRISSIE TOLD HERSELF not to get too excited about this dinner with Ray. After all, he was her neighbor. She had babysat his son, who would be eating with them. It was only natural the two of them should be friends. There was no reason to think he wanted anything more. After all, he was still married, even if he and Tammy were separated. And a man whose wife had left him for someone else wasn't likely to want to rush into another relationship.

When she looked at things from this perspective, she could almost convince herself that Ray was one of the safest dates she'd ever find: a nice man who wasn't in the market for a romance.

But even if all this were true, it didn't negate her own attraction to her handsome neighbor. And this was a beginning. Unless her instincts were completely rusty from lack of use, he was attracted to her, too. Anything could happen, as long as she didn't try to push things along too quickly.

So she resolved to be careful, and brushed her hair, freshened her lipstick, and met him in his driveway, where T.J. gave her a giant hug that melted any lingering reservations she might have had about the evening. She might have her doubts about Ray, but T.J. had long ago captured her heart.

As promised, the restaurant was small and out of the way, tucked into one end of a strip center on the city's south side. "They have homemade ravioli like my mother never made," Ray promised her as he held her chair for her at a white-draped corner table.

"Is your mother Italian?" she asked.

"No, she's just not much of a cook." He grinned at her laughter. "My mother much preferred being on the golf course or traveling somewhere to being stuck in the kitchen," he explained.

"I can't say I blame her there," Chrissie said.

"I don't blame her either," he said. "But as a result I have an exalted view of anyone who can cook. I seem to have inherited my mother's aversion to it."

He seemed to be waiting for her to respond. When she did not, he asked, "So, can you cook?"

She smiled. "I do all right. Sometimes I even enjoy it."

"She makes good mac 'n' cheese," T.J. said.

"Better than mine?" Ray asked.

T.J. nodded.

Ray looked at Chrissie. "I use the same boxed stuff you did. What's your secret?"

She shrugged. For T.J., maybe it really was just a woman's touch, but she wouldn't say that to Ray.

They talked all through the meal, always about trivial everyday things: Chrissie's job, T.J.'s day care, the weather and the price of gas. Anything of consequence—the war, Tammy, Chrissie's late husband—were accepted as off-limits. It made it easier for Chrissie to think of this as just a neighborly dinner, and nothing like a real date.

Stuffed with ravioli, T.J. fell asleep on the way home. Ray pulled his truck into the driveway and cut the engine, but didn't open the door right away. "Thanks for coming with me tonight," he said.

"I had a nice time." She smoothed her hands down her thighs. "Maybe we could do it again sometime."

"I'd like that." His eyes met hers and held, the longing in them stealing her breath and making her want to throw her arms around him and pull him close. Only her awareness of the little boy in the backseat kept her from doing so.

"I especially didn't want to be alone tonight," Ray continued.

A heaviness in his voice captured her attention. "Oh? Why is that?"

He wrapped both hands around the steering wheel, as if he was debating yanking it out of the dash. The muscles of his forearms bunched and tension radiated from him. "When I got home tonight, a letter from Tammy's attorney was waiting for me." He glanced at her, his eyes dark, his expression guarded. "She filed for divorce."

"Oh. I'm sorry." She didn't know what else to say. Had Ray been expecting a reunion with his wife? Was that why he looked so stricken?

"I knew it was coming," he said. "There's nothing left between us, I know that. I just…" He shook his head. "I didn't think it would hit me this way."

"I think…" She stopped, then started again. "I think when two people get married, they go into it expecting the marriage to last," she said. "When it doesn't, for whatever reason, their whole view of life has to adjust. It's like any shock to the system."

He nodded. "Was it like that for you when your husband died?"

"Yes. I expected the grief—the man I loved had died and I understood that was a loss I had to deal with. But I never expected how much I'd mourn the loss of my marriage, too." It was a different kind of loss, but in its own way, just as painful. She'd lost all her dreams of the future—children and grandchildren and growing old with someone by her side. She hoped one day to find those things again but for a while now they'd seemed out of reach, buried along with Matt in that grave at the veteran's cemetery.

"One thing that gets to me is that I thought I knew her so well, and I realize now I hardly knew her at all," he said.

"I don't know if any of us can ever really predict how another person will act," she said.

"We'd only known each other about six months when we got married," he said. "Maybe that's part of the problem."

"Matt and I only knew each other eight months." It was such a short amount of time, compared to how long he'd been gone.

"I met her at a bar, at a place called Shorty's. Do you know it?"

"I've never been there, but I've heard of it." She pictured the long, low building near the base.

He leaned his head against the seat and spoke almost as if to himself. "She was playing pool and I spotted her right off. Something about her grabbed my attention. Then she turned and our eyes met and, I don't know what it was—I never felt that way about a woman before. I thought it meant I was in love."

"Things weren't so sudden for me and Matt," she said. "He asked me out three times before I went with him, and even then, he was always more sure of his feelings than I was."

"When he asked you to marry him, did you say yes right away?" Ray asked.

"No." She smiled, remembering how insistent Matt had been. "But Matt was a good talker. He pointed out that he was going off to fight in a war and it would be better if we married right away instead of waiting. He talked me into it."

"Knowing what happened, are you sorry he did?"

"No. I loved being married to him. I'm grateful for the time we had." Loving him, but not being married to him when he died would have been harder, she thought. As a widow, she had a certain status. A position people understood and respected. She'd seen other young men and women who were only the girlfriends or boyfriends of soldiers who died, and they were sometimes left out of all the ceremonies and activities of bereavement, as if they were somehow less important.

"Tammy didn't want to marry me. Or rather, she didn't want to marry at all. She said she was too young. She was twenty-two. I thought that was old enough."

Chrissie thought of the girl who'd sat in her pajamas all day eating ice cream and watching cartoons. "Some people grow up faster than others," she said.

Ray glanced in the backseat. Chrissie turned to look also. T.J. was still sound asleep. Ray looked up and their eyes met briefly. "Tammy found out she was pregnant about four months after we met," he said. "She wanted to get an abortion—I wanted to get married."

Chrissie didn't know what to say to this, so she kept silent, waiting.

"I knew I'd probably end up in Iraq sooner or later and

I liked the idea of having a family to come home to," he continued. "Maybe it was the age difference—I was already twenty-seven and I was ready to settle down."

"But Tammy wasn't?"

"Obviously not. But I kept bugging her about it and finally wore her down. If I hadn't pressured her, maybe things would have turned out differently."

"You might not have T.J.," she said.

"You're right. And I'm glad I've got him."

"Twenty-two is old enough to settle down and accept the responsibilities of being a mother and wife," Chrissie said. "If Tammy didn't do that, it's not your fault."

"Yeah, you're right there, too. And maybe if I hadn't been away we could have worked things out." He shrugged. "But I was and we didn't, and I have to deal with it and move on."

She nodded. "What are you going to do now?" she asked.

He rubbed the back of his neck. "See a lawyer, I guess. I haven't actually read her divorce petition yet, but I'll want to make some kind of reply, make sure the custody agreement is all in order, though I don't guess that will be much of a problem."

"Have you talked to Tammy at all since you got home?" she asked.

He shook his head. "At this point, I don't trust myself to be civil to her."

"It might be worth it to talk to her, for T.J.'s sake." She glanced back at the sleeping child. T.J.'s chin rested on his chest, hair falling across his forehead. "He's going to have questions someday."

"Yeah." The word came out like a sigh. "I have questions, too, though I don't know if I'm going to like the answers."

He opened the door and she did likewise. "Thank you for the dinner," she said.

"Yeah." He put his hand up, as if reaching for her, then settled for patting her shoulder. "Thanks for everything." Then he turned and lifted T.J. out of his seat.

Chrissie watched father and son trudge up the walk to their front door, her heart fluttering like a captured bird. So much for telling herself not to get involved with him and his problems. One ravioli dinner later, it was already too late.

CHAPTER SEVEN

KNOWING RAY BROUGHT a new energy to Chrissie's life. She woke each morning thinking of him, and timed her exit from the house to coincide with his. They'd stand in the driveway a few minutes, making small talk while their eyes sent messages of longing and desire that left her tingling. The presence of T.J. and the watchful eyes of neighbors kept them chaste, but she smiled all day with the knowledge that Ray wanted her. And when the timing was right, he would have her.

Ray's return home had upset the regular, comfortable rhythm of her life. She realized now she'd been sleepwalking through the days since Matt's death. She'd been comfortably numb, avoiding pain, but not allowing herself to feel much of anything else, either.

Ray had awakened all those numbed senses and dormant feelings. When she was with him, every touch, every look, radiated through her with fierce intensity. Her poor starved libido went into overdrive. She felt like some hormonally overcharged teenager. Something as simple as seeing Ray in the driveway washing his truck, his shirt off, water droplets sparkling in the hair on his chest, was enough to send her into the house with a pounding heart and dry mouth, in need of a cold shower.

She supposed it was an unconventional romance, built on brief conversations and a mutual love for his son that was very different from the dinner and movie dates she'd envisioned. But the mundane everyday exchanges somehow made her feelings for him more real, grounded as they were in reality. At times she was impatient to be alone with him, but she'd waited three years to meet a man like him, so she was willing to wait a little longer, sure the rewards would be worth the delay.

Rita returned to work after a week away. She said little about her visit with Paul and her family, and seemed more subdued than before. Chrissie attributed this to grief, both over her brother-in-law's death and over parting from Paul once more, and didn't press for details.

One afternoon, six weeks after Chrissie's dinner with Ray, after the last patient had been ushered out the door, Rita came and stood in the doorway of Chrissie's office. "Can I talk to you for a minute?" she asked.

"Sure." Chrissie turned from the insurance appeals she'd been reviewing and motioned Rita into the room.

Rita shut the door behind her, then perched on the edge of a chair beside Chrissie's desk. Her face was solemn, a strained look around her eyes that never really left her these days. She'd lost weight, too, the fine bones of her face more elegantly beautiful than ever. "I don't know any subtle way to lead up to this, so I'll just say it," she said. "I'm pretty sure I'm pregnant."

Chrissie caught her breath, then gave a cry of delight and leaned over to hug her friend. "Congratulations. That's wonderful news." Then, seeing that Rita still wasn't smiling, she added, "Isn't it?"

Rita nodded. "We'd talked about starting a family as soon as Paul finished this tour of duty, so I stopped refilling my birth control prescription four months ago," she said. "I didn't even think about it while I was in Pine Ridge."

"Of course you didn't," Chrissie said. "You had a lot of other things on your mind." She touched her friend's hand. "You're happy about this, aren't you? I mean, if the two of you had been planning on starting a family…"

Rita nodded. "I should be happy. I want to be happy. But…" Her voice trailed away.

"But what?" Chrissie prompted.

Rita sighed. "When Paul and I said goodbye in Pine Ridge, things were…tense," she said. "I was upset with him. I still am, I guess."

Chrissie sat back, prepared to listen. "Do you want to tell me why?"

"I need to tell someone. While we were there, I found out that because Paul is his parents' only surviving son, he would be allowed to finish his tour of duty in the United States, instead of going back to the fighting. Of course, that's what I wanted."

What any woman would want, Chrissie thought. But men sometimes saw things differently. "It's not what Paul wanted?" she asked.

Rita shook her head. "No. I don't think he even considered the idea. He said he had to go back, to be with *his guys.*" She knotted her hands into fists. "Then he acted like he couldn't understand why this upset me."

"Of course it upset you," Chrissie said. "You want him home. Safe."

"I thought he'd want to be home, too. To be with me."

The sadness in Rita's voice made Chrissie's throat ache. She squeezed her friend's hand, wanting to offer comfort, but not knowing how.

"It hurts that he'd rather be over there than with me," Rita said, her voice stronger.

"You know Paul loves you," Chrissie said. "Maybe he feels it's his duty to continue to serve with his men."

"Damn duty! He has a duty to me, too, doesn't he? To his family?"

"What do his parents say about it?"

"I don't even know if they know. Even if they did, they would never say anything, except that it's Paul's decision to make."

"Maybe now that he knows you're expecting, he'll want to come home," Chrissie said.

"I haven't told him yet." Rita sat back in the chair and crossed her legs, swinging one foot. "I don't know how. This complicates things."

This puzzled Chrissie. Paul had struck her as the type of man who was devoted to his extended family. The type of man who would make a great father. "You don't think he'll be happy?" she asked.

"I don't know what he'll think," Rita said. "He acted so strange in Pine Ridge. It wasn't just grief—he was so…hard." She looked at Chrissie, sorrow replacing anger once more. "When I looked in his eyes, they were so empty. The Paul I love wasn't there at all. Even when we made love, there was such a distance between us." She pressed one palm against the bridge of her nose, fighting tears. "There's still a distance. He's stopped writing letters. And his e-mails are so—impersonal. It scares me. I know war changes people. How could it not? But I never thought it would change Paul into someone I didn't know."

Chrissie leaned over and took Rita's hand in hers and squeezed it. "Tell him about the baby," she urged. "It will remind him that he has things here at home that are worth coming back to."

Rita nodded. "I'll tell him. Maybe it will make a difference, but I just don't know." She hugged her arms across her stomach. "I always thought the day I found out I was pregnant would be one of the happiest days of my life. Instead I feel so…alone. Scared that things won't turn out right." Her eyes were dark and troubled. "I hate to bring a child into the world when things are so unsettled."

Chrissie hugged her friend close. "Everything will be okay," she said. "Whatever happens, you'll look after your baby and do your best for it. It's all any of us can ever do."

Rita wiped her eyes and nodded and smiled weakly. "They say pregnancy makes woman emotional—I guess in my case it's true." She stood. "Anyway, thanks for listening."

"Congratulations," Chrissie said. "I mean it."

"Thanks."

After Rita left, Chrissie sat for a long time, staring at nothing. Once upon a time, she'd imagined herself as a mother-to-be, learning the good news, announcing it to others, planning for the months ahead. Those thoughts hadn't crossed her mind in a long time, but Rita's news had brought all those old dreams rushing back. She put a hand over her abdomen, wondering if she would ever feel her own child growing inside her.

Resolutely, she pushed the thought away. There was no sense worrying that because something hadn't happened yet it would never happen. She still had plenty of good years left, and a life to live in the meantime.

Rita's confession that Paul had changed worried her as well. He had been one man whom Chrissie would have described as devoted to his wife. Even in the early days of her marriage to Matt, she'd envied her friends' closeness. When Rita entered the room, it was as if an inner light had been switched on in her husband. He often touched her lightly on the back or arm when she was near, as if wanting to maintain a physical contact. Chrissie had always thought that her friends had the kind of marriage she wanted to have one day.

If Matt had returned alive from the war, what would their marriage have been like? They had been very much in love, but untested by the demands of living together day after day. She liked to think they would have remained close, but who could say if that would have happened? The little more than a year they'd been together wasn't much time to get to truly know another person. Though maybe the secret of a good marriage wasn't so much in how long you'd known someone, but how well the two of you adapted and grew together. That kind of closeness took time that Chrissie and Matt had never had.

On the way home she decided to stop by her parents' house. She still couldn't get used to the For Sale sign in the front yard. The flower beds were ablaze with blooming annuals and the front door had recently been repainted.

Inside had the look of a magazine photo spread. Everything was spotless, the recliner had a new slipcover and the air smelled like the vanilla candles her mom now burned constantly. A pleasant smell, but not the complex one that reminded Chrissie of home.

"Chrissie! What a nice surprise." Her mother enveloped her in a hug, then stepped back, smiling. "Will you stay for dinner? I'm roasting a chicken."

"I hope you don't think I stopped by just to get a free meal," Chrissie said.

Her mom laughed. "I don't think that. Though I imagine cooking for one does get old. And you know I always have plenty."

Chrissie followed her mother into the kitchen. She opened the oven door and peered in at a golden chicken in a white Corning pan. The aroma of rosemary and sage made her mouth water. "Is there anything I can do to help?" she asked.

"You can set the table, dear." Her mom opened a cabinet and took down a can of green beans.

Chrissie counted out silverware, then collected three plates from the china cupboard. "Where's Dad?" she asked.

"He stopped by the hardware store to pick up some new hinges for the door into the garage. You know how it's sagged for years. We've got a potential buyer for the house and we want to make sure everything's in top shape for the inspection."

Chrissie tried not to let her mom see how much this news upset her. "Who are the buyers?" she asked.

"A young couple. He works for Coors and she's a teacher. They're expecting their first child and want a bigger place than the townhome they have now."

"That's nice." It was hard to imagine another family eating dinner in this dining room or cooking in this kitchen. "How's work?" she asked, changing the subject.

"Busy." Her mother sautéed slivered almonds in butter and added them to the green beans in a pan. "The maternity ward is as crowded as I've seen it since I've been at the hospital," she said. "All these young families—we're having a mini baby boom."

Chrissie felt a sharp stab of jealousy at these words. She seldom allowed herself to think about babies—how much she regretted that she and Matt hadn't had one, whether or not she'd ever have one. When the longing did surface, she reminded herself she was still young. She had plenty of time.

But then Rita confided she was pregnant, the couple who were interested in her parents' house were expecting and her mother reported on a local baby boom. All her resolve not to worry vanished under this onslaught of reminders that, while everyone else's lives were moving forward, she'd been stuck in neutral, unable to move toward all the things she'd thought she'd have by now. If Matt hadn't died, she'd have two or three children already. Life had cheated her.

She had never wanted grandiose things—fame or wealth or fancy possessions. All she had wanted was a home and family. Simple things that most people took for granted.

"We put a deposit down on one of those patio homes I was telling you about," her mother said as she mashed potatoes. "I can't wait for you to see it. It has the most incredible kitchen. So much room and gorgeous cherrywood cabinets."

Since when had her mom wanted cherrywood cabinets? What was wrong with the painted ones she had?

"You know," her mother said, in the overly casual tone that presaged an announcement about which she'd given much thought. "I've been thinking maybe a move would do you good."

Chrissie blinked, startled. "I don't want a patio home," she said. "I like the house I'm in."

"I wasn't thinking of a patio home." Her mother stirred the beans more vigorously than necessary. "I was thinking it would be good for you to leave Colorado Springs for a while."

"Are you trying to get rid of me?"

"No!" Her mother switched off the burner and turned to face Chrissie. "I know it's hard for you here, with the military base and all the soldiers. I just thought...maybe if you went somewhere else, it would be easier for you to meet a man you could fall in love with." The lines fanning out from the corners of her eyes deepened as she studied her daughter. "I want you to be happy."

"I am happy, Mom." Chrissie squeezed her mother's hands, and swallowed a lump in her throat. "Really, and...and I've started dating again. Nothing serious," she hastened to add. "But he's a nice man. A single dad who lives in my neighborhood." She didn't want to reveal that Ray lived next door, for fear her parents would "just happen" to drop in one day to check him out. Their tentative relationship wasn't ready for that yet.

Her mother's expression relaxed. "That's wonderful." She smiled. "I hope you'll let us meet him soon."

"It's not that serious, Mom," she insisted. "We've only been to dinner once."

"Still, I can tell by your voice that you like him." She turned back to the stove. "And it's so nice to hear you've met someone who can make you smile this way."

Chrissie hadn't even realized she *was* smiling. She touched her lips, surprised to find they were, indeed, turned up at the corners.

"Chrissie's met someone? Who?" Her father came through from the garage and set a small plastic bag on the counter.

"A neighbor," her mother said. "They had dinner together."

"We'll have to meet this young man." Her father frowned. "He is young, isn't he?"

"He's about my age. And it's been only one dinner. It's too soon for you to meet him." Why had she ever mentioned Ray to her parents?

Her mother spooned potatoes into a bowl. "What's his name?" she asked. "What does he do?"

"I don't want to talk about him anymore," she said, taking her seat at the table. "At least let me go on a second date with him first."

"You sound sure there's going to be a second date." Her mother joined Chrissie and her father at the table. "That's a good sign."

Of course there was going to be a second date. Eventually. One thing about the slow progress between them, the time allowed her to indulge in all her fantasies of what might be without worrying about a future that might not be so rosy. She, of all people, knew things didn't always work out the way she wanted. Better to enjoy the exciting anticipation she and Ray shared while it lasted, before real life stepped in and messed things up.

CHAPTER EIGHT

"I CAN'T BELIEVE she has the nerve to ask for custody of T.J. after she deserted us both." Ray gripped the arms of his chair tightly and stared across the desk at his lawyer. When he'd finally gotten around to reading Tammy's divorce petition, he'd been stunned to discover she was asking for full custody of their son. What kind of drugs was the woman taking to think she could get away with that?

"If what you're telling me is true, and your wife has made no effort to contact your son since she left him with your parents almost four months ago, then I'd say your chances of winning a countersuit are good." The lawyer reviewed the notes on the legal pad in front of him. "We could even sue for child support, or for that matter, severing of her parental rights altogether."

Ray shifted in his chair. "I don't know if I want to go that far. I just want to do what's best for T.J." Sometimes he thought it would be better if his son never saw his mother again. But T.J. loved her and missed her and still asked about her, though not as much as he had at first. Was Ray going to be responsible for screwing up his kid for life if he didn't do everything possible to foster some kind of relationship between mother and son? These were the kinds of questions no one ever addressed in those prenatal classes he and Tammy had taken.

"You say your wife is currently living with another man?" the lawyer asked.

Ray frowned. "That's what I hear. Another soldier."

"I can tell you, the courts won't look favorably on a woman who abandons her child."

Abandon. The word made Ray's stomach tighten in pain. "I always thought Tammy was a good mother. She seemed really devoted to T.J. I mean, it was bad enough she left me, but a week doesn't go by that some poor slob over there in Iraq or Afghanistan gets a Dear John letter. But to run out on her little boy..." He shook his head. "It doesn't make sense."

"It won't make sense to a judge either." The lawyer set aside his notes. "I don't think we'll have any trouble getting you anything you want."

What Ray wanted was for this to never have happened. Since that was impossible, he'd settle for it being over with as quickly as possible, and with as little disruption to T.J.'s life as possible. The two of them had developed a comfortable routine. T.J. liked his day care and was coming to accept Ray's cooking. T.J. trusted him now, and hadn't cried for his mother in weeks. Ray wondered if, young as his son was, he might one day forget about his mother altogether.

He and the lawyer discussed a few more details, then Ray wrote a check for the hefty retainer, shook hands and left the office. He'd gotten leave to take a long lunch to keep this appointment and had to get back to the base. But

he had driven only a few miles when his cell phone blared.
He recognized the number from the day care and flipped
the phone open.

The voice on the other end of the line was the receptionist at the day-care center. "Mr. Hughes, I'm afraid T.J.
isn't feeling well. You'll need to come get him."

He cradled the phone between his cheek and shoulder
and slowed for a red light. "What's wrong with him?"

"He says his stomach hurts and it feels like he's
running a fever."

"He was fine when I dropped him off this morning." He
tried to think back, but he'd been rushed, his mind on the
appointment with the lawyer. Was it possible T.J. had been
sick and Ray hadn't even noticed? "He ate his breakfast
fine," he added.

"Sometimes these things come on very suddenly," the
receptionist said. Maybe she was used to reassuring
guilty parents.

"All right. I'll be there as soon as I can. Ten minutes or
so." He flipped the phone shut and switched on his blinker
to exit the freeway and head back toward the day-care
center. When he got there he'd call his commander and
explain the situation. The man had four children of his own
and tended to be understanding about such things.

The boy who greeted him in the administrator's office of
the day-care center was a sad sight, his cheeks flushed, his
head down. "I threw up," he announced in a pitiful voice.

"It's probably just a mild virus." The receptionist, an
African-American woman named Mary, stroked T.J.'s hair.
"There's one going around."

"Do you think I should take him to the doctor?" Ray

studied his son. T.J. obviously didn't feel well, but with kids, how could you know what was really serious?

"Keep an eye on him tonight and see if he's feeling better tomorrow," Mary said. "But remember that he needs to be free of fever for twenty-four hours before he can return to us."

Ray nodded, his mind racing. That meant trying to get leave, or finding someone else to watch him while Ray was on duty at the base. "You ready to go home?" he asked his son.

T.J. nodded and silently held up his arms. Ray scooped him up. He put his hand to T.J.'s forehead. He did feel warm. There was probably a thermometer somewhere in the house, though he had no idea where. Maybe he'd stop on the way home and buy one.

As he buckled T.J. into his car seat, the contrast between the normally energetic little boy and this lethargic child alarmed him. Mary had said to keep an eye on him, but what was Ray supposed to be watching for? What if he had some rare but severe childhood disease like meningitis or something? Maybe Ray should take him straight to the doctor.

Right. As if there was much chance of getting an appointment on a Friday afternoon. And if T.J. really was only fighting a mild virus Ray would have put the boy through all that for nothing.

On the drive home, he tried to remember what his mother had done when he was sick. Mostly, he recalled being left for long hours with only the TV for company. His mother was not someone who was comfortable around sick people, or who had much tolerance for complaints, no matter how justified.

He thought of calling Chrissie and asking her, but rejected the idea. T.J. was his son. He had to learn how to look after him on his own. And he didn't want Chrissie to think he wanted her friendship solely because he needed help with T.J.

One of these days, he'd tell Chrissie how he really felt about her—how much he admired her, how much he enjoyed talking to her and spending time with her, how much he wanted to love her. But a man getting out of one messy relationship had no business trying to start another one. Right now he needed to look after T.J., get through the divorce, then maybe he could think about moving things forward with his neighbor.

He stopped at the store and bought a thermometer, children's Tylenol, ginger ale, Popsicles, Jell-O, canned chicken soup and saltines. He unwrapped the thermometer in the parking lot and took T.J.'s temperature, too anxious to wait until he arrived home. Thankfully, it showed only ninety-nine degrees. Enough to make the boy feel terrible, but not enough to be worried about. With luck, this really would be a passing virus. Maybe T.J. would even be well by morning.

Which still left twenty-four hours before he could go back to day care. Ray would have to try to get leave to look after him.

At home, he tucked T.J. into bed, made soup and carried it into him. "I don't want it," T.J. said, turning his head away.

Ray set the soup on the nightstand and felt his son's forehead. He felt hotter. Maybe he should take his temperature again. But getting T.J. to hold the thermometer in his mouth the first time had been a struggle. He should have sprung for the digital kind he could stick in the ear....

"I've got Popsicles," Ray said. Maybe something cold would cool the boy down. "Would you like one of those?"

T.J. shook his head, his lower lip trembling.

"What would you like?" Ray asked. At this point, if T.J. had asked for a pony, Ray would have done everything in his power to get it for him. If only his son wouldn't look so miserable.

"I want Mama!" T.J. wailed, and burst into tears.

Ray stared at his son and felt utterly helpless. His son wanted the one thing Ray couldn't give him. He tried to pull the boy close and hold him, but T.J. pushed him away. "I want Mama!" he screamed, his face red, tears streaming from his eyes. "Where is she? Why isn't she here?"

"I don't know, son. I'm sorry, I don't know."

T.J. threw himself facedown on the bed and continued to cry, his whole body convulsing with sobs. Ray worried he'd make himself sicker with all this carrying on, but was helpless to stop it. He sat on the edge of the bed and rubbed T.J.'s back. "It's okay," he murmured, over and over. Though he didn't really believe the words.

He wondered if life would ever be okay for them again. Would there ever be a day when things felt normal—when T.J. didn't long for his mother and Ray didn't wonder what had gone wrong with his wife, and what was wrong with *him* that had made her leave them?

At last T.J. relaxed and drifted to sleep. Ray carefully rolled him over and covered him up. Despite his tantrum, his fever seemed no higher, and his breathing was even and regular. Ray hoped in the morning they'd both feel better.

He switched off the light and carried the cold soup back into the kitchen, then went into the living room and turned on the televison. But nothing held his interest. Restless, he paced, one uncomfortable thought after another bombarding him. The call from the day-care center had brought home the fact that he had no real backup system—that if something happened to him, T.J. would be on his own. The knowledge sent a cold chill through him.

Was this how Tammy had felt with him away and no family of her own nearby? Was this what she meant when she wrote she was lonely—not just the fact of being alone, but the fact of realizing that you were responsible for taking care of a child and there was no one else to turn to if something happened? Had the weight of that responsibility been too much for her?

He pushed the idea aside. Such responsibility was part of being a parent. It wasn't something a person could run away from, any more than a soldier would turn his back on his comrades in the middle of a fight.

Some people did run, of course. They were called cowards. Deserters. Ray would never be one of those.

But he resolved to come up with some kind of fallback plan for T.J. He'd start by talking with his parents. Closer to home, he'd ask Chrissie if he could add her to the contact list for the day-care center, in case they were unable to reach him. And he'd teach T.J. that the boy was to go with Chrissie if he ever needed help and couldn't find his dad.

Thinking of Chrissie made him feel better. She was so capable and reassuring.

So genuine and womanly. Every time he was with her he became more aware of her curves, the sweet smell of her hair, the dimples at the corners of her mouth and how thick and lacy her lashes looked. He wanted to stay with her, to listen to the sound of her voice, to bask in the warmth of her smile.

Most of all, he wanted to touch her. To feel the softness of her skin, to cradle her in his arms, to caress her, to feel her body respond to his attentions. He wanted to make love to her, and to feel her making love to him, to connect on a level that went beyond words to something more basic and profound.

He wasn't sure when he'd begun to entertain these fantasies, though maybe they had begun that very first night, when she appeared on his doorstep with a plate of food and a bottle of wine, like a sexy angel ready to appease all his appetites.

It was getting harder to resist the temptation to reach out to her. Two things held him back: his uncertainty as to how she'd respond, and his doubts about the wisdom of getting involved with anyone right now. He was in the middle of trying to untangle himself from one mistake, and he'd heard stories of men getting burned on the rebound. Maybe his feelings for Chrissie were merely a reaction to Tammy's rejection. She was practically the first woman he'd seen once he'd absorbed that blow. Maybe this was just a twisted way for his ego to prove himself.

He'd rushed things with Tammy and that had ended badly. If the attraction he felt for Chrissie was real, it wouldn't suffer for him taking his time.

CHRISSIE WAS AWAKENED early Saturday morning by a knock on the door. She crawled out of bed and stumbled to the door, startled to find Ray standing on the porch, T.J. in his arms. "Do you have to work today at the dentist's office?" he asked, before she could say a word.

"No." She pushed her hair out of her eyes and looked at T.J. The little boy clung to his father's neck and stared at her with sad eyes. His cheeks were flushed, his mouth shaped in a pout. "Is T.J. okay?" she asked.

"He's come down with some kind of virus. Nothing too bad, I don't think. At least, his fever's lower this morning. But I have to be at the base in less than an hour and the day care won't take him until his fever's been normal for twenty-four hours. Can you look after him for me today?"

"Of course I'll watch him for you." She held up her arms and T.J. stretched toward her. She gathered him close and put one hand to his forehead. He was a little warm. "I don't mind at all."

"Thanks. I mean it." He looked at her so long she became self-conscious about standing there wearing only the boxer shorts and T-shirt pajama set her mother had given her last Christmas. "Um, do you have any medicine for him?" she asked.

"Oh yeah." He handed her a paper bag. "There's children's Tylenol in there, and a decongestant. Some Vicks. Throat lozenges. Some cough syrup."

She looked in the bag, eyes widening at the array of pharmaceuticals piled inside. It looked as if Ray had walked down the pharmacy aisle at the grocery store and chosen one of everything. "You didn't give him all of this, did you?" she asked.

"No. Only the Tylenol and the decongestant. But I wasn't sure what I'd need, so I bought it all."

She suppressed the urge to laugh. Ray had a frantic look in his eyes, and dark circles betrayed his lack of sleep. "Were you up all night with him?" she asked.

He nodded. "Most of it."

"Poor baby." She meant T.J., but the words might have been for Ray as well. Except there was nothing babyish about him. He was all hard angles, well-developed muscles and silent intensity. Masculine energy radiated from him and being near him made Chrissie aware of everything feminine within her, as if every part of him complemented some part of her, so that they were perfectly matched.

Which led to the inevitable thoughts of how well they might be matched in the bedroom. She took it as a healthy sign that she'd begun to fantasize about being with a man again, but she wished they were closer to making those fantasies reality.

He shifted and looked away at last. "Thanks again," he said, taking a step back. He reached out and patted his son. "Bye, T.J. I'll see you this evening."

She carried T.J. into her living room. "Let's make you comfortable here on the sofa," she said. She brought pillows and blankets from her own bed and settled them around him. "How do you feel?" she asked.

"Okay." He burrowed deeper into the piles of pillows. "My stomach still hurts a little."

"Do you think maybe some Jell-O would help it?" she asked. "I think I have some. And while it's making, maybe you could have some applesauce."

He nodded.

"All right then. Let me get dressed first. Do you want to watch cartoons?"

With the television on the Cartoon Network, she retreated to her room to dress. The cats followed her, tails switching from side by side, as if to express their displeasure at this disruption of their normal routine. "Don't look at me that way," she told them. "You know you really like him." On his previous visits, both Rudy and Sapphire had spent long hours batting at wads of paper T.J. tossed to them, or swatting at feathers he trailed along on a string. "Maybe later, if he's feeling better, he'll play with you. In the meantime, behave."

Rudy turned his back to Chrissie and curled into a tight ball in the middle of the bed, but Sapphire continued to follow her mistress as she dressed and returned to the living room.

T.J. was sitting up, the remote control in his hand. Instead of cartoons, the television was showing a movie. Chrissie recognized Catherine Zeta Jones and Antonio Banderas in *Zorro*. She leaned over and gently took the remote. "What are you watching?" she asked.

T.J. shrugged. "A movie."

"I thought you wanted to watch cartoons?"

"I did, but…" He shrugged again, gaze still fixed on the screen. "She looks like my mom, doesn't she?"

Chrissie studied the woman on the screen—the long, dark hair, full figure and big brown eyes. Ms. Jones did look like a more glamorous version of Tammy Hughes. "A little bit, yes," she said.

T.J. looked up at her, his face tense with worry. "Is my mom dead?" he asked.

Chrissie stared at him. Her first instinct was to throw her arms around him and hug him close, but she was afraid this would only alarm him. She aimed the remote at the television and clicked it off, then moved around the sofa and sat beside him, all the while trying to regain her composure. "What makes you think she's dead?" she asked.

"Because she left me at Grandma's and she hasn't come back." He sniffed. "Why hasn't she come back unless she can't?"

Chrissie had certainly wondered this, too. Everything she'd seen had indicated that Tammy loved her son. She couldn't imagine staying away from a child of her own this long. "Your mother is not dead," she said.

T.J. leaned close and Chrissie slipped her arm around his slight shoulders. "If she's not dead, where is she?" he asked in a quavery voice.

"I don't know where she is." Chrissie spoke slowly, choosing her words carefully. She wanted to tell the truth, but in a way that would upset T.J. the least. "I don't know why she hasn't called or been to see you," she said. "Maybe one day you can ask her." She looked down at him, wanting to make sure he was paying attention. She needn't have worried. He stared up at her, unblinking, rapt. "Sometimes adults make mistakes," she said. "They do things that don't make sense or are wrong. But whatever your mom has done, I know she loves you very much. She told me so all the time."

"She did?"

Chrissie nodded. "She did."

T.J. snuggled closer. "What else did she tell you?"

"She said she thought you were the prettiest baby ever, and that you were such a good child." She smiled, remembering. Of course, Tammy had said other things. She'd complained about the ordeal of potty training her son, and whined about how having a kid made it difficult to go out and have fun whenever she felt like it. But that had been the immature party girl talking. The mother side of Tammy adored her son, and Chrissie wanted to make sure T.J. knew that.

"I miss her," T.J. said. He cradled his head against Chrissie's side.

"Wherever she is, I'm sure she misses you, too," Chrissie said. How could she not? And if Tammy didn't miss her son, didn't think about seeing him again or when she'd get back to him, then she was a much different person than Chrissie had thought. It was one thing for a woman to leave a husband she hadn't seen in months in favor of a man who was there at the moment. It wasn't honorable or right, but it happened all the time. But for a mother to leave the child she'd loved and raised for over three years was unthinkable to Chrissie.

Not for the first time, envy for all her neighbor had had and so carelessly thrown away filled Chrissie. She would have given anything to be married to a good man like Ray and to have a precious little boy like T.J. What could Tammy possibly have seen in her new lover to make her willing to abandon all she had?

T.J. yawned loudly.

Chrissie glanced at him. "Are you sleepy?"

He nodded. "I didn't sleep good last night."

"Do you want to take a nap?"

He nodded again, then looked up at her. "Sometimes Mama used to rock me to sleep," he said. "Could you do that?"

Her throat tightened and she had to swallow sudden tears. "Sure. I can do that." She gathered him in her arms and carried him to the rocking chair across the room and sat. Folding a knitted afghan around them, she rocked and hummed softly under her breath—lullabies her mother had once sung to her. After a while, T.J. relaxed in her arms and his breathing became deep and regular.

She continued rocking, holding him, indulging in smelling his hair, enjoying the comfortable weight of him in her lap, how well her arms fit around him. Rita was right—she was meant to be a mother.

Maybe—that small glimmer of hope that had been building inside her grew a little brighter. Maybe one day she could be T.J.'s mother, if she and his father could find a way to express all these feelings that simmered inside them.

RAY RETURNED that evening with Chinese food. "I thought the least I could do was provide dinner," he said, holding up the bag.

"You didn't have to do that." She took the bag from him and carried it into the kitchen. The aroma of sesame chicken and egg rolls made her mouth water. "It smells delicious, though."

T.J. ran and threw his arms around his dad. Ray hoisted him in the air. "You look like you're feeling better," he said.

T.J. nodded, smiling.

Father and son followed her into the kitchen. "He had a long nap this morning," Chrissie said as she unpacked the various cartons and tubs and transferred the contents to plates and bowls. "When he woke up, his fever was gone and he ate a bowl of soup and another of Jell-O. We spent the afternoon reading, watching television and playing games. He beat me twice at Old Maid."

Ray laughed. He was clearly more relaxed now than he had been this morning. And even more dangerous to her equilibrium. Black stubble showed along his jaw, giving him a rugged look that screamed red-blooded, red-hot male.

They ate at the kitchen table, T.J. insisting on using chopsticks until he ended up wearing more food than he ate. Ray cleaned him up while Chrissie repackaged the leftovers for the guys to take home.

"Let me help you with the dishes," Ray said when he returned from the bathroom, a scrubbed T.J. in tow. "I'll get T.J. settled on the sofa." The little boy looked ready to nod off again any minute.

"All right," she agreed. "Why don't you open a bottle of wine?" It was probably dangerous to let down her guard so much with him, but she was feeling more reckless than usual, maybe the results of an entire day when the man before her had never been far from her mind.

Ray returned to the kitchen a moment later. "He feels a little warm, but maybe that's just from his bath."

"I think he'll be fine in the morning." She handed him the wine bottle and a corkscrew.

He opened the wine and poured two glasses while she filled the sink with soapy water. "So it went okay today with you two?" he asked as he handed her a glass.

She leaned against the sink and sipped the wine. "It went fine," she said.

"I was wondering." He contemplated his wineglass, slowly turning it in his hand. "I need to ask you a favor."

His sudden somberness surprised her. "What is it?"

"I need someone to be my backup at the day care. Someone they can call in case they can't reach me."

"Of course. I'd be happy to do that. Anytime. T.J.'s a wonderful boy." Her voice trailed away, remembering how sad he'd been when he talked about his mother.

"There's something you're not telling me," Ray prompted.

She could hear the television in the next room, T.J. laughing at the copy of *Aladdin* she'd inserted in the DVD player. "He asked me if his mother was dead—if that was why she hadn't been back to see him."

Ray looked like a man who'd been punched in the gut. He set aside his glass and folded his arms across his chest. "He said that?"

She nodded. "I guess to his way of thinking, the only reason his mother would have left him was if she wasn't *able* to come back."

Ray wiped his hand across his face, fingers cupping his jaw. "What did you tell him?"

"I told him she wasn't dead. That I didn't know why she hadn't been to see him, but that I knew she loved him and missed him. I hope it's true."

He stared at the floor, shoulders hunched. "There's a special hell for anyone who'd do this to a kid," he said finally.

Chrissie said nothing. Maybe he was right. And maybe Tammy was already in that hell. Or maybe she really was more heartless than any of them had guessed. Chrissie turned to the sink and began washing dishes.

Ray moved beside her and picked up a towel to dry. "It would be easier if she was dead," he said after a minute.

"I know you don't mean that," Chrissie said.

He sighed, a heavy sound. "I tracked down her address a couple of days ago," he said.

She stared at him. "You did? You talked to her?"

"No. I found out her new address and drove by there."
He dried a glass, held it up to the light as if inspecting for
spots, then set it on the counter. "My truck was in the
driveway. My old truck. The one she stole."

Chrissie winced. "Did you see her?"

He shook his head. "No. But I saw a man. I guess the
new boyfriend." He frowned. "He's tall and skinny and
looks to be all of twenty-five, if that. A boy."

"I'm sure you don't want to see her, and I can't blame
you for that," Chrissie said. "But I think it would be good
for T.J. if he could see her." Maybe if he saw his mother
was all right and talked to her, he wouldn't be so sad.

"She's asked for full custody of him."

The bowl she'd been washing slipped from her fingers.
"How could she do that, after leaving the way she did?"

He shook his head. "I'm countersuing, asking for full
custody myself. I don't think she'll win, but it's one more
delay in getting all this settled."

"At least it proves she wants to see him again." Her
feelings were in a turmoil. As a woman, she sympa-
thized with Tammy wanting to be a part of her son's life,
but she also keenly felt the hurt her actions had caused
father and son.

"I don't know if I like that idea," Ray said. "What if she
rejects him again? Seems like she made it pretty clear she
doesn't want either one of us in her life."

"I think Tammy doesn't know what she wants."

She thought about all the things she wanted, things
Tammy had had and thrown away—children, and a home
with a good man. *This* man. They locked eyes, and the intensity of his gaze pinned her against the counter. Looking

into his eyes was like staring into a deep, dark lake, a place that looked placid but one she knew was filled with all sorts of hazards.

And yet, she was drawn to those depths, like a diver for whom the pull of undiscovered treasure was greater than her fear of danger.

He hesitated, then bent and pressed his lips to hers. She stood on tiptoe, leaning into him. She'd been anticipating this contact, imagining it, wanting it, even as she dreaded it, for so long that she was reluctant to pull away anytime soon.

Ray responded to this encouragement by pulling her closer, opening his mouth slightly and urging her lips apart. His tongue swept across her lips, gentle and enticing. She put one hand up to steady herself and it seemed the most natural thing in the world to thread her fingers through the hair at the nape of his neck, and to lean closer still.

His beard stubble scraped her cheek, and he tasted of the wine they'd drunk together. This was heaven, this soaring, wild feeling that overtook her.

He was the first to move away, straightening and continuing to stare into her eyes. "I've been wanting to do that for a while now," he said. "It was even nicer than I expected."

She could only nod, dumbstruck. The kiss had been more than nice. She felt as if she was floating, the moment surreal: the sound of cartoons from the next room, the smell of Chinese food still lingering in the air, the very ordinary setting for an onslaught of such extraordinary feelings. Her heart pounded and her cheek still burned where his beard stubble had scraped it.

"Dad!"

The cry from the other room made them pull farther apart. Ray glanced over his shoulder, then back at her, regret heavy in his eyes. "I'd better go," he said.

She nodded, and followed him into the living room.

"What's up, sport?" Ray asked his son.

"Can we go home?" T.J. asked. "I'm sleepy."

"Sure." He gathered the child into his arms, and Chrissie walked them to the door.

"Thanks for dinner," she said.

"Thank you. For looking after T.J., and for listening to me."

"I'll look after him anytime. All you have to do is ask." And she would listen to him anytime as well. Though she kept this thought to herself.

"Good night." He bent and kissed her again, a brief brush of his lips against hers that nevertheless sent another jolt of heat through her. "Thanks again," he said, then walked off into the night.

She stared after him, wondering if she'd dreamed this whole episode. Had Ray really kissed her? She touched the sensitive skin of her lips. If this was a dream, it was the most realistic one she'd ever had.

She smiled, happiness bubbling through her. Now she knew Ray shared these feelings they had never put into words. There was a future for them, one she could look forward to, one that would be made up of more than dreams and fantasy. It was only one kiss, but it held the promise of so much more.

CHAPTER NINE

T.J. BOUNCED BACK quickly from his illness and returned to day care on Monday as if nothing had ever happened.

Ray didn't recover so quickly from the kiss he and Chrissie had shared. The pull between them as they stood so close together, alone at last in her kitchen, had been too strong to deny. If T.J. hadn't interrupted them, he might have gone further, pressing her against the counter and making love to her the way he'd too often fantasized doing.

It was probably just as well T.J. had stopped them. When she'd opened her mouth to him, a storm of emotion had overtaken him—everything from outright lust to a deep longing that troubled him. Was his reaction due to the fact that he'd been alone so long—or was it because Chrissie was such a special person?

Of course, he'd believed Tammy was special, too, and he'd been wrong about her.

He hated that Tammy's departure left him doubting himself and his judgment this way. All these cascading side effects of her leaving felt even worse than his initial sense of betrayal. Knowing she'd hurt T.J. was the worst pain of all.

He'd meant it when he told Chrissie it would be better for T.J. if his mother were dead. Knowing she was gone forever had to be easier to accept than wondering why she'd left and if she'd show up again one day.

No matter how Tammy felt about Ray and their marriage, how could she have done this to T.J.? Maybe Ray ought to go talk to her. He had fully intended to confront her the day he drove over there.

But, when he'd seen his own truck sitting in the driveway, the bottom had dropped out of his stomach. The memory of his first night home from Iraq had slammed into him, engulfing him in the black despair he'd felt when he'd stared into his empty garage and felt stripped of everything he'd ever wanted or loved.

He'd had to drive away then, afraid of what he might have done to Tammy had he seen her. Or worse, that he might have embarrassed himself by falling apart in front of her.

But he'd had time to pull himself together now, and vowed to find some time this week to go back and talk to her. He'd be fine with her never entering his life again, but he figured for T.J.'s sake, he'd better try to find out what was going on with her.

There were guys in Iraq who swore that focusing on the bad things too much would bring them to your door. A guy who obsessed over IEDs would find one with his name on it in a street or alley he was patrolling before too long. Short-timers with only a few days before their flights home became paranoid, fearful a sniper or bomb would take them out before they had the chance to leave. They couldn't stop thinking about the possibility, yet believed focusing on it would make it come true. They were snagged in a trap, afraid to say or do anything.

Ray wondered if that sort of magical thinking was

preying on him when he pulled into the driveway that evening and found his truck—the one Tammy had taken— sitting in the driveway. At first he wondered if she'd decided to return it, then he saw the woman standing beside it.

"Mama!" T.J. shouted, and began fumbling with the latch of his booster seat before Ray had even come to a stop.

Ray shut off the engine and turned to help T.J., avoiding looking at Tammy. As soon as he released his son, the boy hurtled to his mother and threw himself into her arms. Tammy knelt and held him close, smoothing his hair and talking to him. Ray watched them, hands in his pockets, trying to figure out what he was going to say to her. What he could say in front of T.J.

His first impression was that she looked so young— younger than he remembered, or was it only that he'd been blind to how much of a girl she still was? She'd cut her hair, so that it hung in spiky layers to her collarbone, with streaks of reddish blond through the brown. She was wearing a sleeveless gauze top, half a dozen silver brace-lets, jeans and platform sandals. When she looked up at Ray, he was surprised to see there were tears in her eyes.

The tears did not move him. "Come to return the truck you stole?" he asked.

She flinched, but quickly recovered. One hand on T.J.'s head, she stood and faced Ray. "I needed a vehicle and my name was on the title. I knew you'd want me to have it."

"You knew that, huh?"

Her gaze darted away. T.J. tugged at her shirt. "Mama, I learned a new song in school. Do you want to hear it?"

Her smile was bright for her son. "Sure I do, honey."

While T.J. sang "Little Bunny Foo Foo" and giggled wildly every time he pantomimed bopping field mice on the head, Ray watched Tammy watching her son. He tried to find something different about her—something hard and ugly that would explain the hard and ugly way she'd acted. But she looked the same as she always had—a beautiful girl, her hair, nails and makeup perfect. She was a woman used to being the center of attention, a woman accustomed to other people making accommodations for her and not the other way around.

No wonder waiting for him to come home from the war had been so trying for her. Tammy wasn't used to waiting for other people; they had always waited for her. And up until he'd been shipped out, Ray had been the same. *He'd* pursued her in their relationship. *He'd* begged her to marry him. He'd bought the house she chose and made sure she never had a chance to be bored and unhappy.

And then he left her to look after herself and their son and everything fell apart.

When T.J. had finished singing, both parents applauded, then Ray put a hand on his son's shoulder. "Why don't you go in the house and get that drawing you made in school the other day to show your mom?" he said.

"Where is it?" T.J. asked.

"It's in my bedroom. On the dresser."

T.J. raced into the house, the door slamming behind him. When he was out of sight, Ray turned to Tammy. "What are you doing here?" he asked.

She folded her arms. "I wanted to see my son."

"After all these months, you suddenly decided you missed him?"

She pressed her lips into a thin line. "I had some things I had to take care of first. And I knew he was safe with you."

"He's safe all right. And I'm going to keep him that way—safe from whatever head games you're playing with him."

"Don't talk to me that way."

"What did you expect, when you come waltzing in here after all this time?"

"I told you, I had things I had to see to first. But now that's all settled and I can look after him again."

The words made Ray's blood turn to ice. "I'm looking after him. He doesn't need you."

She tossed her head, like a willful horse, or a model posing for a photographer. It was a move designed to draw attention, Ray saw now. Part of the way she'd lured him in. "Don't be ridiculous," she said. "Of course he needs me. I'm the one who looked after him while you were gone for more than a year. I've only been away a few months."

"He asked the other day if you were dead."

Her face paled. "Why would he ask that?"

"He couldn't understand why else you'd leave him. Frankly, I couldn't either. But I understand now. It's because you've always put your own wants and desires ahead of anyone else's, even your son."

"That's not true!" Her voice rose. "I left him with your parents because I couldn't take him with me right away. I knew he'd be safe there. But now I have a place for him and there's no reason he can't come with me."

"There's a big reason. I won't let him. I'm raising him now."

"And what are you going to do when you have to go back to the war? At least he'll know I'm not going to leave him again."

"He'll know no such thing. You did it once—why wouldn't you do it again?"

She glared at him, and opened her mouth to answer, but the front door slammed again and T.J. ran up and handed her the crayon drawing of the princess he'd made. Tammy studied the picture and blinked rapidly, her eyes bright. "Oh, sweetheart, that's so beautiful." She hugged him close. "I'm sorry I've been away so long," she said. "But I'm back now. Are you ready to come and live with me?"

Ray took a step toward her before he even realized he'd moved. When he looked down, his hands were clenched. But he didn't let out the shouts that crowded against his lips, for fear of upsetting T.J., who had already been upset enough.

The question clearly confused the boy. "You live here with me and Daddy," he said.

Tammy smoothed T.J.'s hair back from his forehead. "I used to, but I live in another house now. And I've fixed up a room there just for you. You'll like it, I promise. And we can see each other every day."

T.J. looked over his shoulder at Ray. The confusion in his eyes galvanized Ray into action. He scooped the boy into his arms and glared at Tammy. "T.J. lives with me now. This is his home. You're the one who chose to leave us."

She narrowed her eyes and reached for her son, but Ray took a step back. "I think you'd better go now," he said.

She glared at him, then hitched her purse more firmly

on her shoulder. "I'd hoped we could talk about this civilly, but I guess now we'll let the court decide," she said.

"I guess we will."

She turned and climbed into the truck—*his* truck—and cranked the key so hard the engine made a horrible, grinding noise. Ray tightened his grip on T.J. and watched her drive away. He was so angry, he was literally shaking, and decided he'd better go inside before he dropped T.J. or squeezed him too tightly.

T.J. looked after his mother also, his bottom lip jutted out and starting to tremble. "Why did Mama leave?" he asked.

"She had to go back to her new house." He carried T.J. into the living room and dropped onto the couch, the boy still in his arms.

"Why didn't she stay in this house with us?"

He looked into his son's eyes and struggled to find the right words. How did he explain this whole situation to a three-year-old when he didn't really understand it himself? "Sometimes, mommies and daddies can't live together anymore," he said.

The lines creasing T.J.'s forehead deepened. "Why not?"

"Because, for a man and a woman to live together, they have to love each other. Your mother and I loved each other once, enough that we even made you. But…sometimes things happen and people…well, they grow apart. They don't love each other anymore. So they can't live together anymore."

The boy's expression remained clouded. Ray felt helpless, but he plunged on, trying to find the right words to reassure his son. "The important thing to remember is that I love you very much, and I'll never stop loving you."

"But you stopped loving Mama?"

"Yes. Sometimes that happens with mommies and daddies. But it never happens with parents and children."

"It doesn't?"

"No. I'll never stop loving you." He hugged T.J. to him, trying not to squeeze too hard, resisting the urge to crush the child against his chest, to hold him tightly and never let him go.

"I love you, Daddy," T.J. said in a wet, quavering voice.

"I know, son." He patted his back.

"I love Mama, too."

"I know." He sighed.

"Will I see her again, soon?"

He wanted to say no. He didn't want to see his son torn apart by Tammy drifting in and out of his life at will, or by his parents battling over him. "We'll work something out," he said. "So you can live here with me and sometimes visit with your mother."

He definitely did not want to see the boy living with Tammy—and with her new lover—full-time. But if she was serious about being a part of T.J.'s life again, he didn't see how he could legally keep her away. She might not like it, but he was pretty sure a judge would see things his way. In her own way, he was sure Tammy did love her son. But that didn't mean she would take better care of him than Ray. She'd let the boy down once. He wouldn't give her a chance to do it again.

CHRISSIE LEFT WORK on Tuesday preoccupied with the list of items she needed to buy at the grocery store on her way home. As a result, she didn't notice the woman in the big red truck parked next to her car. But when the door of the truck opened and Tammy stepped out, Chrissie could only stare.

"Hi, Chrissie," Tammy said, offering a shy smile. "Long time no see, huh?"

"Tammy!" Chrissie clutched her purse and stared at her former neighbor. Tammy had a new haircut and was maybe a little thinner, but other than that she looked the same—same stylish clothes, perfect makeup and easy attitude. She certainly didn't look like a woman who felt the least bit guilty about deserting her husband and son. "What are you doing here?" she asked.

"I wanted to see you. I was hoping we could go somewhere for a drink or something."

"Thanks, but I really can't." Chrissie moved closer to her car. The last thing she wanted was to spend time socializing with Tammy.

"Please? Just one drink." Tammy's tone was plaintive. "I really need to talk to someone and you always gave me such good advice."

None of which you ever listened to, Chrissie thought. But curiosity got the better of her. She wanted to know what Tammy had been doing for the past four months, and maybe gain some insight into why she'd left in the first place. "All right. Just for a little while."

"Great." Tammy's smile was brilliant. "There's a great place down the street, The Palms. Do you know it?"

Chrissie nodded. She knew the bar, though she'd never been inside. "I'll follow you there."

Tammy was obviously well-known at The Palms. The bartender and two of the waitresses greeted her warmly when the two women entered the dark wood-paneled tavern. "Hey, Frank," she called to a handsome young man behind the bar. "Fix us two of your fabulous margaritas, would you?"

Chrissie had intended to stick to Diet Coke, but then again, maybe a little alcohol would help her get through this conversation.

They settled into a corner booth and a waitress soon brought over the drinks, along with a basket of snack mix. Tammy scooped a handful of the mix onto a napkin and picked through it with one long, pink-painted fingernail. "I guess you think I'm a pretty awful person," she said.

Chrissie sipped her drink and didn't answer. What could she say?

"You can't think anything worse about me than I've already thought about myself," Tammy continued. She selected a peanut and popped it into her mouth.

"Why did you leave the way you did?" Chrissie asked.

Tammy looked up and the women's eyes briefly met before the younger woman returned her gaze to the table. "You probably won't believe me, but I was in love," she said. "Really in love. Kurt's a great guy. Funny and kind and…and we have fun together."

That was her definition of love—having fun together? Sure, fun was important, but love and marriage were about so much more. "Are you saying you left Ray because you stopped having fun?" Chrissie asked.

Tammy had the grace to wince. "I liked Ray," she said. "I really did. We had some good times. Then I ended up pregnant. I wasn't ready to settle down. To be a mom. But he flipped out when I suggested an abortion." She stirred her drink. "I'm glad I didn't do it now. I love T.J. so much. But I was scared."

Chrissie could understand that, a little. When she was Tammy's age she hadn't been ready to be a parent either.

"Ray convinced me everything would be all right," Tammy continued. "He'd take care of us. So we got married. And we were happy. We had T.J. and things were great. We went out and had a good time together, and we had our son."

She fell silent again, picking out peanuts and eating them, one by one, her brilliant white teeth crunching down on them. She sighed. "Then Ray went off to Iraq and there I was, stuck in that house with a baby, nowhere to go, nothing to do. It made me crazy. So I started going out. It made me remember how much fun I'd had when I was single—and it seemed so long since I'd enjoyed myself like that. I met Kurt." She looked across the table again. "He's a great guy, Chrissie, he really is," she said. "I didn't mean to do it, but the next thing I knew I'd fallen for the guy. It surprised me—it really did. He's not as good-looking as Ray or anything. But there's something about him." She put her hand over her heart and got a dreamy look on her face.

"You loved him enough to leave Ray and T.J.?" Chrissie had a hard time believing this.

The dreamy look vanished, replaced by an angry pout. "I wasn't leaving T.J. Not permanently. But Kurt lived in this crappy little apartment in a not-so-good neighborhood. In order to get a nicer place, I had to go to work to earn money. I didn't have anywhere for T.J. to sleep and no one to look after him. So I sent him to Ray's parents. I knew he'd be fine there, and then when he got home, Ray could look after him until I was ready for him to move in with me."

"You stayed away four months with not a word," Chrissie said. "That's a long time to a little kid."

Tammy shifted in her chair and stirred her drink again. "I knew it would be hard on both of us if I saw him and then had to leave, so I made myself stay away. It wasn't easy, you know. But I was thinking of him. Putting him first."

She made everything sound so logical, in a twisted way. So sensible. Except she'd obviously never taken into account anyone's feelings but her own. "Weren't you worried about him?" Chrissie asked. "That he'd feel abandoned? That he'd miss you?"

"I missed him, too. So much. But it was only for a little while." She shrugged. "Kids that little don't remember much anyway. And at least I wasn't leaving for a year, the way Ray did."

"Ray didn't have much choice."

"Well, yeah. But still." She wet a fingertip and used it to blot salt from the rim of her glass, then sucked on it. "Anyway, Kurt and I have a great new place now, with a fenced backyard and everything. I found a woman who will look after T.J. for me. It'll be great."

"Except that T.J. is used to living with his father now," Chrissie said. "Another change might not be good for him."

Tammy straightened and frowned at her. "Hey, whose side are you on?" she asked. "Everybody knows little children need their mothers. Besides, you can't say Ray is a really dependable father—not when any day now he could get orders to go back to Iraq for another year or fifteen months or longer. If he's got custody of T.J., what's he going to do?"

Chrissie didn't like this reminder that Ray could be sent back to the fighting. She'd been avoiding thinking about that. "There are other single parents who are soldiers," she said. "They all manage to make arrangements. And he has his parents."

Tammy looked more agitated than ever. "But the point is, *I* don't have to worry about any of that. And I'm T.J.'s mother."

"I've seen T.J. with his father," Chrissie said. "They're very attached to each other."

"Despite what you might think, I'm not a total bitch," Tammy said. "I'd still let them see each other. I was going to tell Ray all that, but he freaked out on me."

"You've already talked to him about this?" Chrissie gripped her glass, not even feeling the cold. Ray must have been enraged when Tammy showed up after so many months of silence.

"I talked, but he didn't listen. He said he wanted full custody of T.J. That's ridiculous."

Chrissie pressed her lips together, fighting the urge to reach over and shake the younger woman. "What is he supposed to think?" she asked. "He came home from the war and you'd moved out, took most of the furniture and his truck, and dumped his son off at his parents'. That isn't the behavior of a devoted mother."

"I told you why I did what I did," she said, her voice rising in a loud whine. "I picked out all that furniture, so why shouldn't I take it? And the truck was in my name.

My car had been towed and I had to have transportation. And I only left T.J. until Kurt and I could get more settled."

"Does Ray know about Kurt?"

Tammy's gaze slid away. "I'm sure he does. I mean, I didn't mention him or anything, but word gets around."

"And you don't think all this behavior will make you look bad in court?"

She shook her head. "I'm his mother. And Ray isn't a saint, you know. I'm sure he's already sniffing after some other woman. Men like him don't stay single long."

Chrissie flinched, but kept her expression calm and made no comment. Tammy sucked on her straw, making loud gurgling noises as she drained her drink. "What about you? Are you dating anyone?"

Chrissie's face felt hot. "No one in particular." After all, she and Ray weren't exactly *dating*.

Tammy pushed her glass aside. "Talk to Ray for me," she said. "Try to persuade him not to fight me on this."

"Why should I do that?" Chrissie asked.

"Because you're my friend."

She was more Ray's friend than she'd ever been Tammy's, but she couldn't say that. Not without Tammy wanting to know more details than she was willing to reveal.

"I know he's upset with me," Tammy said. "But try to make him see this is best for T.J. He needs his mother and the stable life I can give him now. Kurt and I plan to get married as soon as my divorce from Ray is final, and we'll probably have more kids some day, so T.J. will have brothers and sisters."

"Ray might remarry one day as well." Her chest felt pinched as she said the words.

"Is he seeing someone?" Tammy looked smug. "I'll bet he is. Women were always all over him. I'd be standing right there and they'd still come on to him. Can you believe it?"

Chrissie could believe it. Ray was not only good-looking, he radiated a confident strength that made a woman feel she could rely on him. "I don't want to take sides in this," she said.

Tammy reached out and put her hand over Chrissie's. "Then don't do it for me. Do it for T.J. I know you were always crazy about him."

She nodded. "I can ask Ray to do what's best for T.J. And I do believe you should be a part of your son's life." It would be too devastating to T.J. to be abandoned by her again.

The waitress stopped by their table. "Another round?" she asked.

Tammy shook her head. "I have to go."

"Then I'll leave the check." The waitress laid the bill facedown on the table between them.

Tammy rummaged through her purse and came up with a five-dollar bill. "That's all I have on me," she said, laying the bill atop the tab. "With all the expenses of setting up a new place, things are really tight right now."

Chrissie said nothing, but added a ten to cover the rest of the bill and a tip.

"I was wondering…" Tammy studied Chrissie across the table. "Maybe you could lend me some money? Just to tide me over, you know?"

"How much money?" Chrissie asked.

"A hundred dollars would be great."

A hundred dollars! Chrissie coughed. "No, I can't do that."

"Fifty? Even twenty would be great."

She shook her head. "No, I don't think so."

Tammy shrugged. "Okay." She slid out of the booth. "Talk to Ray for me, okay? Make him see the sense in this."

Then she slung her purse over her shoulder and sashayed out of the bar, men throughout the room turning to watch her exit.

Chrissie sat and finished her drink. She contemplated ordering another, then decided against it. She was less certain what to do about Tammy. On one hand, she didn't like what Tammy had done. And she knew how much Ray loved his son, and how angry he was at his wife.

But she also knew how much T.J. missed his mother. How often he had cried for her. He still needed her. Ray couldn't give him the woman's touch he needed. And Chrissie was only a next-door neighbor, a poor substitute.

She'd talk to Ray, she decided. She'd get his side of the story. And try not to let her personal feelings for father and son get the better of her.

CHAPTER TEN

RITA'S HEART BEAT a little faster as she logged on to her e-mail account. She scanned the list of messages in her in-box, searching for Paul's screen name, and bit her lip to keep from crying out when it wasn't there. Messages from him were rare as silver dollars these days and her disappointment at yet another evening without one was crushing.

He said he'd been too busy to write much, but Rita knew something besides the demands of his job kept him from her. His handwritten letters had stopped altogether, replaced by infrequent e-mails and rare sessions of instant messaging when she managed to catch him online.

She checked the clock and did the math necessary to determine what time it was in Baghdad. She thought Paul had told her he often got off of patrol about now. She signed into her instant-messaging service and said a silent prayer.

Her heart leaped when she saw the symbol indicating that Redman27 was online. With shaking hands, she typed in her message.

RedRita: Hello sweetheart! How are you?

She waited, holding her breath, until his answer appeared.

Redman27: Hey. I had a free minute and just sat down.

RedRita: It's good to hear from you, even online.

Redman27: Yeah. So wassup?

RedRita: I had the first sonogram today. Everything looks good.

She paused, then added: I wish you could have been there. Our baby is beautiful.

She'd cried when she'd seen the shadowy form on the screen, tears of joy and amazement, and regret that she was seeing this without Paul by her side.

Redman27: That's good.

RedRita: I'll send you the pictures as soon as I can scan them in.

Redman27: That's okay. I wouldn't know what I was looking at anyway.

Disappointment cut deep. She'd hoped tangible proof of their child's existence would stir some enthusiasm in him. But whenever she introduced the topic, he changed the subject.

As he did now.

Redman27: AJ got hit yesterday. IED. He's in Landstuhl. Don't know if he'll make it.

A.J. Wright was a member of Paul's team, a younger man whose early enthusiasm for the war had both amused and annoyed Paul.

RedRita: I'm sorry. I'll pray that he makes it okay.
Redman27: Yeah.

As she stared at the blinking cursor on her screen, she could feel him pulling even further away. Where was the man who had been so eager to share the news of his life in Iraq with her, who had joked and encouraged her across the miles—the man who had poured his heart onto pages of crisp stationery, his neat handwriting forming a lifeline between them? When Matt had died, Paul had taken it hard, but he hadn't let his grief come between them. Since Jeremy's funeral he'd been replaced by this terse, distant stranger.

Redman27: Listen, I'd better go. Other guys are waiting to use the PC.
RedRita: Wait! Paul, I really need a little more of your time tonight. Please.

She stared at these words for long seconds, until her eyes ached from not blinking. The icon showed he was still online.

Redman27: What is it?
RedRita: What is going on with you? Why are you so distant?

Another long wait. Was he angry with her? Damn him if he was. How could he expect her to go on like this, with him giving her the cold shoulder and her not knowing why?

Redman27: Excuse me if I'm a little preoccupied. War has a way of doing that.

RedRita: Just remember, the war is not your life. Your life is here with me.

It was something he had told her over and over again in the early days of his tour.

Redman27: The war is my life now.

She blinked hard, refusing to cry anymore. And she refused to let him off with that.

RedRita: You haven't asked about the baby. Aren't you happy about him?
Redman27: It's hard to be happy about bringing a kid into this f****d up world.

The profanity startled her. It wasn't Paul's style, at least not around her. She typed faster than ever, her fingers hitting the keys hard, as if she could telegraph the intensity of her feelings with each keystroke.

RedRita: Then our job is to make sure the world isn't so messed up. And our child might be the one to make a difference.
Redman27: I don't know if anything can make a difference at this point. We're supposed to be making a difference over here but most days I can't tell that we are.

It was one of the longest—and most emotionally revealing—sentences he'd written in weeks.

RedRita: You sound down. You've been through a lot. Maybe you should talk to someone about it.

Redman27: You mean a shrink. I don't need to waste my time with one of those headshrinkers. I just need to stick tight with my men and get through this.

RedRita: You can always talk to me. Anytime.

Redman27: This is something I have to get through on my own.

Rita ground her teeth together. It was so typical. Macho man, didn't need any help. Didn't need a woman's sympathy. The independence and toughness she admired in her husband could also be the things that made her the most crazy.

RedRita: Just don't shut me out. Remember I love you.

Redman27: Love you too. I really do have to go now.

RedRita: Take care. Write soon.

Redman27 has signed off.

She stared at the message for a long moment. Paul had signed off, all right. He'd signed off of communicating with her, of expressing any feelings about the baby they'd once eagerly anticipated. He'd signed off of his life outside the war zone—the life he had once said was the only thing keeping him sane amid the chaos of Iraq.

It was as if when Jeremy died he took part of Paul with him. Rita didn't know how to get that part back—how to get her husband back. But she had to keep trying, for Paul's sake, for the sake of their marriage and for the sake of the child she carried. Their baby deserved to know the wonderful, loving man Paul had been. The man he would be again, if she could only find a way to reach him.

"WHAT DO YOU MEAN, she might succeed in taking T.J. from me?" Ray paced his bedroom, struggling to keep his voice down so that T.J., who was splashing in the bathtub in the next room, wouldn't hear.

"Not take him from you, but certainly if his mother can prove she's capable of providing a stable home for him, a judge would be amenable to granting her partial, or even full custody." The lawyer's voice was calm and reasonable, as if he were discussing the details of a real estate transaction. Meanwhile, Ray was shaking with barely suppressed rage.

"She deserted him," he said, his voice cracking. "She left him with my parents and didn't bother to see him or speak to him for months."

"The judge will definitely take that into consideration. But I can guarantee her lawyer is going to focus on the care she took of him for the year you were away, and prior to that. And he's going to point out the fact that you could be redeployed at any moment and emphasize the instability of your situation as compared to the home life she can provide."

"She's living with the guy she left me for," he said. "The man she left *him* for. Whose side are you on anyway?"

"I'm on your side. But the only way we'll win this thing is to consider every angle her attorney is going to present to the judge. Then we come up with a defense."

"So what's my defense?"

"We emphasize the care you've given your son in the past three and a half months, the bond you've built, any financial advantage you might have. Are you dating anyone?"

He thought of Chrissie, and the kiss they'd shared. But he couldn't call the few meals they'd shared real dates. Caring for a three-year-old and the demands of both their jobs and everyday life made it tough to find time for them to be alone together. "No," he said. "I'm not dating anyone."

"Then don't. In the eyes of the court, you're still a married man. Right now we have the moral high ground. We don't want to lose it. As far as the judge is concerned, we want him or her to see you as the devoted father who's too busy looking after his son to have anything but the most chaste relationship."

Which was pretty much the truth, though lately his thoughts around Chrissie hadn't been all that chaste. "Gotcha," he said. "No fooling around."

"Exactly. Now, what about visitation for the mother?"

He thought of the joy in T.J.'s eyes when he'd seen Tammy again. "Visitation is okay," he said reluctantly. "T.J. still needs his mother."

"What about shared custody?"

"No."

"You might want to consider it. It will be much easier to win the judge over on that, and if you are redeployed, T.J. would have somewhere familiar to go."

"No." He didn't want to ever leave T.J. again, but if he had to, he didn't want it to be to Tammy and her new boyfriend and the uncertainty there would always be over whether or not she would run out on him again. "She's proven she can't be trusted. I won't put T.J. through the emotional wringer that way."

"All right. Have you thought any more about child support?"

"What about it?"

"As custodial parent, you're entitled."

"I don't think Tammy has any money." When he'd met her, she'd been working behind the counter at an auto glass shop. He had no idea what she was doing now, but she didn't qualify for any skilled position.

"We'll ask for the minimum then."

"I don't care about the money, I just want my son."

"The money's important, too. If not for you, then for T.J. You can put it aside to pay for his education."

"Whatever. I just want my son."

"I get the message. Listen, try not to worry. I'll talk to you in a couple of days."

Ray hung up the phone and sagged onto the bed. *Try not to worry.* As if he'd done anything else since Tammy had walked back into his life and asked to see T.J. He listened for a moment to the splashing from the bathroom. T.J. was singing a song about boats and from the sounds of things, creating his own tidal wave.

Ray went into the bathroom, where he found T.J. wearing a soap-bubble beard, a washcloth draped over his head like a makeshift beret. "Come on, sport, time to rinse off," Ray said, dodging a puddle and picking up a towel.

T.J. splashed off the soap suds and climbed out of the tub. "When can I shave, like you?" he asked as Ray toweled him dry.

"A long time," Ray said. He tried to imagine the little boy in his arms as a gangly young man sprouting chin hairs and found it impossible. He was only beginning to know his son as a little boy. He'd just as soon stave off the rebellious teen years a while longer.

He helped T.J. into pajamas, then carried him to the bedroom. T.J. chose *Where the Wild Things Are* for his bedtime story and Ray read it, doing his best funny voices, rewarded with T.J.'s giggles. This nightly ritual comforted him even more than it did T.J., he thought. It was a familiar routine that brought each day to a satisfactory close, a constant he could look forward to, no matter what else happened during the day.

He tucked T.J. into bed, kissed him good-night and switched off the light, then retreated to the living room. Away from the soft glow of T.J.'s puppy-dog night-light, loneliness and uncertainty crowded around Ray.

Such emotions had been familiar companions in Iraq. On nights when he felt the worst, he'd focused on his family the way he'd been trained to fix his attention on the markers that noted the narrow safe zone of a minefield. Those markers—and the wife and child waiting for him back home—were what would get him safely home.

When he'd received Tammy's letter, telling him she wouldn't be waiting for him anymore, he'd thought he'd lost all that. But he'd been wrong. His son was the strongest tie of all. T.J. needed him to look after him and keep him safe. But in a way, T.J. also kept Ray safe—kept him sane and grounded in a way he'd never been when he was single.

A knock on the door startled him, and he checked his watch. Eight-thirty. Late for a visitor. He checked the peephole and was surprised to see Chrissie waiting on his doorstep, her face cast in shadow by the porch light. His chest felt tight as he remembered the first night when she'd stood on his doorstep, so unexpected and beautiful he'd wondered for a moment if she was a hallucination— a sign that he truly was cracking up.

He jerked the door open. "Chrissie."

"I know it's late, but may I come in?"

"Sure."

He held the door open wider and she moved past him, the faint floral scent of her drifting over him, sending a jolt of desire through him.

She stood to one side, hands twisted together, shoulders hunched, tension radiating from her. "Is everything okay?" he asked, his own anxiety mounting.

She looked around the room, as if searching for something. Or someone. "Where's T.J.?" she asked.

"He's in bed. Asleep."

She looked at the floor.

"Can I get you something to drink?" he asked.

She shook her head. "No, thank you."

He wanted to demand that she tell him what was wrong, but restrained himself, waiting for her to tell him on her own. "Why don't we sit down," he said and led the way to the couch.

She sat beside him, and he took her hands in his, a gesture as natural as picking up his son when he'd fallen. Her fingers were ice-cold, and he squeezed them gently between his own. The thought occurred to him that this was not what his lawyer had meant when he'd advised him to live like a monk.

But the situation was innocent, even if his thoughts weren't.

"What's wrong?" he asked again.

She took a deep breath and looked at him, her eyes dark with worry. "Tammy came to see me this afternoon. She came to my office."

"What did she want?" He didn't even realize he'd been squeezing her hands until she winced. "Sorry." He released her and sucked in a deep breath, trying to stay calm. "What did she say?"

"She wanted me to talk to you—to ask you not to fight her on her request for custody of T.J."

"Why would she ask you that?"

Chrissie shrugged. "I guess because she knows we're neighbors—and she thinks of me as her friend."

"And are you her friend?" He tensed, waiting for her answer, remembering his accusations the first night they met—that she was the one who led Tammy astray. He believed Chrissie hadn't been responsible for that—so why did her answer matter so much to him now?

"I tried to be her friend," Chrissie said. "But we were never really close. I don't feel as if I even know her now."

"I know what you mean. I thought I loved her and now she's a stranger to me." He glanced at her. "What did you tell her?"

She raised her head and met his gaze, her eyes filled with concern. "I told her I would encourage you to do what's best for T.J."

"And what do you think that is?"

She looked away again, and worried her lower lip between her teeth. "I know Tammy has her faults, but she was a good mother to him—at least until she met this new man and ran off. I know T.J. loves her and I think he'd suffer if she wasn't part of his life."

Ray stiffened. He had hoped that Chrissie, of all people, would take his side in this. She knew what Tammy was like. "I don't intend to cut her out of his life altogether," he said. "She can have visitation."

Chrissie didn't look any less worried. "What will you do if you get sent back to Iraq?" she asked.

"I'll manage." How, he had no idea. He could ask his parents to take T.J., but they were liable to say no. "I need to make arrangements," he said. "I want to be able to prove to the court that I can provide for him."

"I know you want the best for him," she said. "That's what I told Tammy." She put her hand on his. "I know you love T.J. very much. And he loves you. As much as children need their mothers, they need fathers, too."

Some of the stiffness went out of his shoulders. He should have known Chrissie wasn't taking sides in this. "My lawyer says the fact that Tammy left might not mean as much as the fact that she came back. And my being subject to redeployment could hurt my chances of being awarded full custody."

"What are you going to do?" she asked.

"I'm going to fight as hard as I can," he said. "T.J.'s been through enough already—he shouldn't have to leave his home, too." He took another deep, steadying breath. "My lawyer says right now I have the moral high ground, so I have to do my best to maintain it."

She nodded, but said nothing, her gaze once more on the floor.

He studied her again, the curve of her cheek, the way her hair curled around her ear, and wanted nothing more than to press his mouth to the soft skin of her neck, to close his eyes and inhale her fragrance, to feel her arms reaching around him. He wanted to hold her and be held, to lose himself in making love with her. He had to grip the sofa cushion hard to keep from reaching for her. "You know if things were different, I'd ask you out," he said. "But I can't right now. My lawyer says I have to live like a monk."

The only acknowledgment that she had heard him at all was the rosy blush that warmed her cheeks.

"If I asked, would you say yes?" he prompted.

She plucked at a loose thread on the hem of her blouse. "Yes," she said. "Yes, I would." She looked at him with the expression of a woman determined to be brave in spite of every feeling to the contrary. It was a look he knew well from the day his unit had shipped out, when most of the wives, girlfriends and mothers wore variations of this same expression.

"Since we can't date, we probably shouldn't talk about it," she said. Her smile was a brief flutter of her lips upward before they resumed their downward turn. "We can still be friends. It's better that way."

Better than what? he wanted to ask. He couldn't imagine that friends would be better than lovers; he hoped to have the chance to one day find out, but who knew how long that would be? In the meantime, he needed all the friends he could get. "I'm glad to have you for a friend," he said.

Her smile was brighter this time, more genuine. "I'm glad you're my friend, too."

Again, he fought the impulse to kiss her, settling instead for a brief brush of his hand against her arm. Then he stood, and thrust his hands into his pockets, needing to distance himself from her. "You'll let me know if you hear from Tammy again?"

She stood also. "I'll let you know." She hesitated, then added, "There was something else she asked me, which struck me as a little odd."

"What was that?"

"She wanted to borrow money. She asked for a hundred dollars at first, then lowered the amount to twenty."

He frowned. "Did you give it to her?"

She shook her head. "She was dressed nicely, and driving your red truck, and she said she was working, so I don't know why she'd have needed the money."

"Whatever job she has, it probably doesn't pay that much. As for the clothes, she was always particular about her appearance." It was one of the things that had drawn him to her, the fact that she was so stylish and fastidious. He'd mistaken this attention to detail as a sign of maturity, rather than the vanity it was.

"Yes, she always took care with her appearance," Chrissie said. "I'm sorry about your truck. Maybe I shouldn't have mentioned it."

"No, I'm glad you did. It could be useful information." At her look of dismay, he added, "Not that I expect you to spy for me or anything."

"I doubt if I'll see her again," she said. "I don't think she was too happy with me when I turned down her request for a loan, after I'd refused to plead her case to you."

He walked with her to the door. "Thanks for stopping by tonight," he said. "It felt good to talk to someone about this."

"Anytime," she said. "I've always been a good listener."

She looked up at him, her head tilted at the perfect angle for a kiss.

He took a step back. "Well, good night."

"Good night."

He held the door for her, then closed it behind her, and stood for a long time with one hand on the doorjamb, head bent, listening to the rapid thud of his heart. Now he had one more reason to resent his soon-to-be ex-wife. If it weren't for Tammy, he'd be able to pursue the one woman who'd awakened his battered libido and made him consider the possibility of love again.

He straightened and squared his shoulders. No sense dwelling on what couldn't be. For now he had to put the knowledge of what he needed to do for his son ahead of what he needed for himself as a man.

CHAPTER ELEVEN

AUGUST HIT Colorado Springs with soaring temperatures and cloudless skies. Chrissie tried to blame her restlessness and irritability on the heat, or on her anxiety over her parents' impending move. But she knew the majority of the blame lay with her handsome next-door neighbor, whose acknowledgment of his attraction to her had stirred a storm of emotion within her that had not calmed in the weeks that followed.

She'd been both flattered and dismayed by Ray's admission that he wanted to date her, and both relief and disappointment had battled for the upper hand when he'd announced that, for now at least, they could be no more than friends. Friends was what she wanted, wasn't it? But no sooner had he set that boundary, than she couldn't stop remembering the one kiss they'd shared, and imagining what it would be like to have more than a kiss from him. She felt like a high school girl, pining after what she couldn't have, wanting what she knew wasn't good for her.

Her distraction seemed to be contagious. Allison was flighty and forgetful, and Rita misplaced equipment and became uncustomarily clumsy. "I'm sorry," she apologized when she dropped a newly sterilized tray of instruments. She sank to her knees and began gathering up the items. Her long hair fell forward, shielding her face, but as Chrissy reached for a dental probe, a single tear fell to the floor.

"Rita, what is it?" Chrissie turned to her friend. "It's only a bunch of instruments. We can run them through the sterilizer again."

Rita shook her head and gathered up the last of the tools. "Don't mind me," she said. "Everything makes me emotional these days." She pushed back her chair and smiled, too brightly, then shoved to her feet. Her pregnancy was just beginning to show beneath her pink scrubs that were the office uniform.

"Are you sure everything's okay?" Chrissie asked. She couldn't ever remember seeing Rita cry before; were hormones really all that was to blame? "Is Paul okay?"

Rita shook her head. "Paul is… I don't know what he is."

Chrissie took the tray from Rita and led her by the arm into her office. "There are tissues on my desk. I'll take these to the prep room and get you some cold water."

"Thanks." Rita sniffed and dabbed at her eyes. "Sorry I'm such a mess."

"You don't have anything to apologize for." Chrissie left and returned quickly with a cup of water, and slid into a chair across from her friend. "I lost count of all the times you gave me a shoulder to cry on after I lost Matt. What's up with Paul?"

This question led to a fresh stream of tears, which Rita tried vainly to stem by blotting her eyes with a tissue. She sniffed and shook her head. "I'm so mad at him right now—and afraid for him." She grabbed up the cup and gulped water, then blew her nose. "I found out he volunteered with a team whose job is detonating unexploded IEDs."

"You mean, like a bomb squad?"

Rita nodded. "He *volunteered* for this craziness. As if Special Forces isn't dangerous enough!"

Chrissie shuddered. Improvised Explosive Devices were the number-one cause of injuries and deaths in the war. Volunteering to set off those that had been discovered unexploded seemed a job for someone who was either foolhardy or a daredevil. Paul had never seemed to her to be either of these things. "Did you ask him why he did it?" she asked.

Rita nodded. "He said they needed someone. I told him he should leave that kind of duty to single men who didn't have children and he got really upset." Her voice grew quiet. "He asked if I meant men like Jeremy—if they were the only ones who were supposed to make any real sacrifices." She gulped. "That made me even angrier. I told him I knew if Jeremy were alive, he'd tell him not to be such an idiot. He said I didn't know what I was talking about and signed off."

Chrissie put her hand over Rita's. "I'm sorry," she said.

"We can't even have a decent fight because of this damn war." Rita shredded her tissue. "If Paul was here in front of me, maybe I could figure out what's going on with him." She looked at Chrissie. "He's been acting strange since Jeremy died. Does he think because his brother made the ultimate sacrifice, he has to prove he's as brave or tough or…or *something*…as his little brother?"

"He'll be home in a couple of months," Chrissie said.

"He'll see you and the baby will be real to him and things will get better, I'm sure."

"I keep telling myself to hang in there, but then something like this happens and I want to reach out and shake him—to make him be the old Paul I love again."

"He will be, once he's home again." At least, she prayed it would be so.

"Let's not talk about it anymore." Rita pulled a fresh tissue from the box and blew her nose. "Tell me what's been going on with you. Are you still seeing that good-looking neighbor of yours?"

Chrissie's face suddenly felt hot. "I'm not *seeing* him," she said. "Except to say hello across the driveway. And I looked after his little boy once when he was sick and couldn't go to day care."

"Uh-huh. And he brought in takeout and you had dinner together again."

"Nothing happened." Except one unforgettable kiss. Which wouldn't be repeated. "He's getting a divorce and fighting for custody of his son. His lawyer told him not to date anyone."

"So you're waiting for that to blow over and then you two will be an item?"

Chrissie shook her head and straightened a stack of files that didn't need straightening. "I don't know what will happen." Not knowing was part of the problem. Her life felt stuck in limbo once more because of a man. This time not because she'd lost one, but because she couldn't have one—yet.

"He sounds like a man who would be worth waiting for," Rita said.

"Why do you say that? I mean, I haven't told you much about him."

"You've told me enough." Rita leaned forward, her expression serious. "And you should see yourself when you talk about this guy. He's not some soldier who tried to pick you up in a bar or an ordinary neighbor who stopped by one day to borrow a cup of sugar."

"I don't know what you're talking about." But her face felt hotter than ever.

Rita sat back, her gaze still fixed on Chrissie. "I'm glad you've found someone, even if you have to wait for him. I know you've been lonely since Matt died. And you deserve to be happy."

"I don't know if happiness is something people deserve or don't deserve." She sighed. "But it's definitely something I want." Was Ray a man who could bring her happiness? She hoped so, but how could she be sure? She forced a smile. "Don't worry about me. I'll be fine."

"I hope that thanks to Captain Hughes, you'll soon be *very fine.*" Rita waggled her eyebrows and grinned, then slipped out the door when Chrissie came after her.

Chrissie let Rita go, and returned to her desk, though as usual she was unable to focus on work. Was Ray *the one*—the man she'd be happy with for the rest of her life? Her heart fluttered at the thought, and she felt shaky all over. Ray was a wonderful man—a good father, loyal and smart with a sense of humor. And she was definitely attracted to him physically. That didn't mean he was someone special, did it?

But would an ordinary neighbor haunt her dreams and daydreams the way Ray did? Would any other man make her giddy at the thought of running into him when she came home from work each evening?

And would the thought of a casual acquaintance returning to Iraq, where he might be injured, or even killed, make her feel so panicky and afraid, the way the idea that these things could happen to Ray did?

She closed her eyes and took a deep breath, fighting for elusive calm. She didn't want to think too much about what all these feelings meant. She didn't want to accept that it might already be too late for her—that she might have already gone and lost her heart to a man she couldn't afford to love.

AFTER SEVERAL WEEKS of negotiations, Ray's and Tammy's lawyers had brokered an agreement allowing Tammy weekly visitation of every other weekend and Wednesdays on the weeks she didn't see T.J. on weekends. Perhaps fearing trouble, she requested the weekly transfer be conducted at a neutral location.

Which was how Ray found himself on a hot afternoon in early August with T.J. at a family counseling center not far from the base, awaiting Tammy's arrival.

Ray held tightly to T.J.'s hand as they settled into two chairs in the room to which they'd been directed by a stone-faced receptionist. He tried not to let his son see how upset he was, not only at surrendering T.J. for the weekend, but with having to do it at this place, as though he couldn't be trusted. "You know my phone number, right?" he asked the boy.

T.J. nodded and repeated the number.

"And you know if you need anything at all while you're at your mom's, you can call me? Anytime."

T.J. shifted in his chair, his feet dangling. "I'm not supposed to use the phone by myself," he said.

This must be something Tammy had taught him. Ray clenched his jaw, then forced himself to relax. "We'll make sure your mom knows it's okay for you to call. And you know how to dial nine, one, one in an emergency, right?"

T.J. nodded. "We learned about that in school."

Ray sat back in his chair and tried to relax. A painting across from them showed a group of children on a playground. They all looked happy and normal, far removed from anything Ray felt right now.

"What are you going to do while I'm away?"

This sounded like more than an idle question, as if T.J. was really worried about his dad. *Besides wander around an empty house and wonder how it came to this?* Ray thought. *Besides worry about what you're doing and whether or not you're happy?* He forced a smile. "I'll be fine. I'll probably just watch TV and catch up on some chores."

T.J. nodded, though he didn't look any happier. Ray thought about asking if T.J. wanted to go home. They could walk out now and drive away before Tammy showed. He'd call his lawyer and tell him the boy didn't want to go, and that it wasn't right to force him.

The door opened and Tammy rushed in.

"Mama!" T.J. hurtled from the chair to his mother's arms. She knelt to gather him close, holding him tightly for a long moment. Ray looked away, feeling small and petty. So much for thinking T.J. didn't want to see his mother.

"How are you, Ray?"

Her voice was soft, the same voice that had charmed him so much when they first met, with its breathy quality and faint Southern accent. The fact that he still felt its charm angered him, and his answer was brusque. "You're late. I was about to give up and leave."

"Only five minutes," she said, standing but continuing to hold T.J. close. "I just got off work and you know how the traffic is on Friday afternoons."

She was dressed plainly for her—a short dark skirt and white blouse. Almost like a uniform. "Where do you work?" he asked.

"The Steaksmith. I worked the lunch shift today."

The Steaksmith was an upscale restaurant with an expansive bar. Was she a waitress or hostess or bartender? He was curious, but didn't want her to think he cared.

But she was no longer looking at him. She smiled at T.J. "I have the whole weekend off. We're going to have such a good time together."

Ray moved away from them and stared out the room's one window, which faced the parking lot.

"Don't worry," she said. "I'm alone. Kurt is at the base."

He hadn't realized he'd been so obvious, looking for the other man. If he had his way, T.J. would never meet the guy, but Ray couldn't do anything about that, could he?

He turned from the window and picked up the small duffel T.J. had helped him pack that morning. "Here's his stuff. I put in a couple of his favorite books. He likes a story before bed. And he likes bubble bath."

She laughed. "It's not like I've forgotten about my own son," she said. "He and I have spent more time together than the two of you have."

Right. She knew all these precious little things he'd had to discover on his own. He and T.J. had been two strangers who had formed a bond and he couldn't help fear she was going to do her best to destroy all that. Wasn't that what a custody battle was all about—each side trying to prove he or she is the better parent? The one the child needs most?

Tradition seemed to be on the side of the mother in that argument—she was the nurturer who, after all, had given birth.

But did T.J. need a mother who had run out on him? And why wasn't anyone asking how much Ray needed his son?

"Here's my number," he said, handing her a small card. "I told him he could call me anytime if he needs anything or even if he just wants to talk."

She shrugged and tucked the card in her purse. "Sure. My lawyer gave you my number, right?"

He nodded. "And your address." He looked around the sterile meeting room. "I don't see why I couldn't have just dropped him off there."

"I didn't want to take a chance of you starting something with Kurt if he was home."

He bristled at the implication that he couldn't control his temper. "My concern is for T.J.," he said. "Not you or Kurt." Ray had asked around, trying to find out more about Private Kurt Schneider, but all he'd learned so far was that he was assigned to a support group and had not seen duty overseas yet. If Ray ever caught him alone, he might very well smash his face in, but he'd never do so in front of T.J.

"It's only for a little while anyway," Tammy interrupted his thoughts.

Her confidence angered him. Shouldn't she be a little

more repentant—grateful even, that he hadn't fought her attempt to get visitation? He hadn't fought it because his lawyer had assured him he'd probably lose, but she didn't need to know that.

She met his gaze, her expression somber. "Kurt tells me he heard a rumor the Sixth Cav might be redeployed soon."

"That's a lie." He'd only been home a few months, too soon to be shipped back.

She shrugged. "It's what he heard. If it's true, I think everyone will agree it's better if T.J. comes to live with me."

Everyone as in the courts. He was aware of T.J. watching them, eyes wide, and forced himself to take a deep breath and to speak calmly. "I don't think we should talk about this now," he said.

"You're right." She turned to T.J. "You ready to go?" she asked, smiling.

He glanced at Ray. "I guess so."

Ray patted T.J.'s back and manufactured a smile of his own. "You go on and have a great time, son," he said. "I'll see you before you know it." After all, it was only one weekend. They could get through one weekend. Somehow.

"Let's go, then," Tammy said.

They signed out with the receptionist, who still hadn't cracked a smile. Ray followed the mother and son to the parking lot, and was startled to see Tammy was driving a faded blue Dodge Neon. "What happened to the truck?" he asked.

She pressed the button on the remote to open the trunk. "I don't have it anymore."

"What do you mean you don't have it anymore? Did something happen to it?" His voice rose.

"Don't make a scene, Ray."

He forced himself to lower his voice. "I'm not making a scene. I just want to know what happened to it."

"I sold it. I didn't really need something so big and I used some of the money to pay my lawyer." She dropped T.J.'s bag in the trunk and slammed it shut, her expression defiant.

His stomach knotted and anger choked him, but he knew better than to say anything. Nothing would come out sounding civil and he didn't want to upset T.J. He focused on the boy, who still looked apprehensive, and very small, clutching the purple teddy bear, Mr. Pringles, tightly to his chest. "You have a good time this weekend, sport," he said, bending to give the boy a quick hug. T.J. felt so small and fragile in his arms. It was all Ray could do not to sweep him up and carry him away.

Instead, he stood and took a step back. "I'll see you Sunday afternoon."

Then he turned and walked away, afraid to look back.

In Iraq he'd had to interrogate veiled women while they wept over dead children. He'd carried the bodies of dying comrades to medical care, and driven through hot zones holding his breath, believing that every minute could be his last. But nothing he had done was harder than walking away from his son now.

He left the parking lot ahead of Tammy and turned toward his house, driving automatically, all his thoughts on his son and his ex-wife. He was almost past the liquor store when he decided to stop, slamming on the brakes and swerving into the parking lot accompanied by the honking and cursing of the driver behind him.

Once inside the store, he grabbed a six-pack of beer and carried it to the register.

"Hello, Ray."

He turned and blinked at the woman in line behind him, sure his mind was playing a nasty joke on him. But no, there stood Chrissie, a bottle of wine in her hand. Was she destined to always appear before him like this at his worst moments? "Hello," she said again. "Is everything okay? You look upset."

The line moved forward and he set his beer on the counter. "I just dropped off T.J. to spend the weekend with Tammy," he said.

Her smile crumpled. "I'm sorry. I know that's really hard." She set her bottle of wine behind the six-pack. "But you know he'll be okay."

He nodded. "I hope so. I don't know anything about this guy Tammy lives with. And I don't know how T.J. will like being away from home."

"He'll do okay," she said. "Probably better than you. Children have a way of living in the moment and not worrying about things that might or might not happen."

He took out his wallet and paid for the beer. "I guess you're right."

"What are you going to do this weekend?" she asked as the clerk rang up the wine.

He held up the six-pack. "This is as far as I've gotten."

"Maybe you shouldn't be alone."

"What are you doing?" He eyed the bottle of wine. It was an expensive brand. The kind of thing she might buy for a fancy dinner with a new boyfriend. The thought made his throat tighten. He cleared it and added, "Are you alone?"

"I'm going over to my parents' to help them finish packing on Sunday." She accepted the bagged bottle of wine from the cashier. "This is a housewarming gift for them."

"But tonight you don't have plans?"

She shook her head. "Nothing special."

Some of the tension in his chest loosened. "Want to have dinner with me?" he asked.

She looked startled at the invitation, then wary. "I thought your lawyer said you shouldn't date."

He held the door for her and followed her into the parking lot. "I'm legally separated now. I doubt if anyone would think it immoral of me to have dinner with a woman. But who said anything about a date? I asked you to dinner. We've eaten together before." Though never without a three-year-old chaperone.

She unlocked her car door, not looking at him. He was prepared to step in front of her if necessary, anything to keep her from leaving. She deposited the wine in the passenger seat, then glanced up at him. "All right," she said.

He blinked. He'd been so prepared to have to work harder to convince her. "Then you'll go with me?"

She nodded. "Sure." She glanced up at the sky. "It's a beautiful evening. Why don't we have a picnic?"

"A picnic?" He felt like an idiot, repeating her words this way, but his mind was suddenly stuck in low gear, unable to react quickly.

"Sure. We can stop by the grocery store and grab food from the deli."

"Where would we go?"

"How about Garden of the Gods?" She leaned closer, her voice lowered. "It will be more private than a restaurant. I know you think it's all right if we're seen together, but I don't want to do anything to make things harder for you in court."

He nodded, touched by her thoughtfulness. "All right." The Garden of the Gods was a national landmark on the west side of the Springs that featured ancient rock formations in a tranquil setting. A romantic setting, even. "I'll follow you," he said. "And thanks. I was dreading going home to that empty house."

Her smile was sad. "I know what you mean. This will be much better. At least for a little while."

She got in her car and he walked to his truck and prepared to follow her. He'd put off his sadness and worry a few hours longer. Chrissie gave him something different to focus on, and maybe the chance to find out, once and for all, where the two of them were headed.

CHAPTER TWELVE

EQUAL PARTS COMPASSION and passion had led Chrissie to agree to Ray's dinner invitation. He and T.J. had become so close, she knew he was in for a rough time, this first weekend apart. But more selfish impulses drove her as well.

A picnic seemed a safe enough way to test their attraction. They'd be in a public place, but with enough privacy to have a real conversation. And the outsize scale of the rock formations at the Garden of the Gods seemed a good way to put her fears into perspective.

They stopped at a grocery store, where she selected bread, chicken fingers, pasta salad, grapes and chocolate brownies. Ray insisted on paying, then added plastic plates, wineglasses and a corkscrew. "I'll buy you another bottle of wine for your parents if we can drink yours tonight," he said.

"All right." The idea of savoring the expensive cabernet herself, rather than giving it away, was temptingly indulgent.

They drove in two cars to the park. While he carried the food, she grabbed an old quilt from her trunk and they walked up the pink sandstone trail that wound among the red rock monoliths. They passed a trio of climbers scaling the face of one formation, and crowds of tourists snapping photographs of balanced rocks and pink-and-white cliffs.

"Where are we going?" Ray asked as they left most of the crowds behind.

"One of my favorite places," she said. She led him through a maze of pathways to a gap between two towering rock monoliths. They emerged into a shady oasis of green grass and flowering shrubs. Though they could occasionally hear other people nearby, this niche seemed set aside from the rest of the park. Chrissie spread the quilt and began to set out the food while he opened the wine.

"How did you know about this spot?" he asked.

"I was visiting the park with my best friend, Celia, and she showed it to me." She hadn't thought about Celia in a long time; the two of them had had a lot of adventures together, all instigated by the mischievous blonde who had lived across the street until both girls were in high school. "Our parents were frantic when they discovered we'd disappeared, but I loved having my own secret hiding place." She hadn't even gotten around to showing this place to Matt; there hadn't been time before he died.

Ray handed her a glass of wine. "Here's to secret sanctuaries," he said, touching his glass to hers.

Sanctuary. A place of safety. But she wasn't sure she felt safe here with Ray. He was no threat to her physical safety, of course, but the man definitely endangered the quiet, safe life she'd built for herself since Matt's death. Though, was it safety she'd found since then, or merely a rut?

"So you grew up in the Springs?" he asked as they helped themselves to the food. "Has it changed much?"

She nodded. "It was a much smaller town when I was a girl. It's always been a military town, of course, with Fort Carson and the Air Force Academy right here. There are a lot of new housing developments, more shopping, new businesses. But it's always been home to me."

"Do you have any brothers and sisters?"

"I have an older brother who lives in Houston and another in Grand Junction. What about you?"

He wiped his fingers on a paper napkin. "I'm an only child."

She imagined him as a boy, with T.J.'s winsome smile. "Were you a spoiled boy?" she teased.

He shook his head. "My parents are not the coddling type. In fact, I sometimes felt like more of an inconvenience to them than anything else."

He said the words so matter-of-factly, but she felt the pain behind them. "Why would you think that?" she asked.

He picked at the crumbs of brownie on his plate. "Before I was born, they traveled a great deal and I temporarily put a stop to that," he said. "As soon as I was old enough to leave by myself, they took off again."

"How awful for you."

He shrugged. "It made me self-reliant. But I swore no child of mine would ever be made to feel that way."

"You don't have anything to worry about. You're a wonderful father to T.J. He adores you."

"I'm pretty crazy about him." He set aside his empty plate. "Which I guess is why it was so hard to leave him today."

"Did he seem okay with spending the weekend with his mom?"

"I think he was looking forward to it. He was certainly glad to see her. If anything, he was more worried about leaving me."

Of course he was. T.J. was such a special child. "That's so sweet."

"Yeah." He drained his wineglass. "I deserve an Academy Award for the acting job I did, telling him I'd be okay."

"I suppose parents get used to it after a while," she said. "I mean, so many share custody or visitation these days. And the kids seem to adapt."

"I guess so." He sighed, but didn't look any happier.

She studied him for a moment—the tight line of his mouth and stiff set of his shoulders. She sensed there was more to this story, something he hadn't yet said, but maybe needed to say. "Did everything else go okay?" she asked.

"She sold my truck."

"Your truck?"

"The one I bought before I left for Iraq. I'd just paid it off before I shipped out, and she took it with her when she left."

"She sold it? If it was yours, how could she do that?"

"The title was in her name. I thought I was making things easier for her by doing that. You know, in case anything happened to me."

"Why did she sell it? Did she say?"

"She said she needed the money to pay her lawyer." He plucked at a plume of grass and slit it with his thumbnail. "She's driving a secondhand Neon. And she's working at the Steaksmith." He tossed the grass aside. "I know it's stupid to get so upset about a vehicle, but it was like…I don't know, like getting rid of that truck was her way of getting rid of the last symbol of our marriage. As if she was saying I didn't mean any more to her than that truck did. She used me for a while, then got rid of me, the way she did the truck."

Did his words hurt so much because Chrissie felt such empathy for him, or because she hated knowing he still loved Tammy enough that she could hurt him this way? "I'm sorry," she said. She looked down at her plate and picked at a grape. "If it's any consolation, I doubt Tammy sees it that way. From what I know of her, she often acts on impulse. She probably got a bill from the lawyer, looked around and saw the truck and decided selling it was the answer." She wondered sometimes if such cold practicality weren't a better approach to life, instead of the sentimentality that made change so hard for her.

"You're probably right." He refilled both their glasses. "I guess that's not the only thing that's upset me."

"Oh? Did something else happen?"

"She said her boyfriend heard a rumor my unit's going to be redeployed soon."

Chrissie suddenly felt sick and her hand shook so much she had to set her glass aside. "Do you think that's true?"

He shook his head. "Of course it's not true. We've only been home a few months. No unit gets sent back that soon."

Of course he was right. Then again, in the early days of the fighting, soldiers had never stayed in Iraq more than a year before being sent home. Recently deployment had been extended to fifteen months. Maybe the time home was being shortened as well.

"I think she said it to get a rise out of me. I complained about having to meet her at the family counseling center and she said it wouldn't be for long anyway, that if I got shipped out again, *everyone*—meaning the court—would realize T.J. was better off with her."

Was Tammy really that mean and manipulative? "So you really think the rumor isn't true?" she asked.

He popped a grape into his mouth and crunched down hard, then swallowed. "No way. I'm not even going to think about it anymore." He leaned back on his hands and smiled at her. "I'm having a picnic on a beautiful summer evening with a beautiful woman. I'd be a fool to waste that time worrying about some lame attempt to upset me."

She returned his smile. "You're right. It's too nice an evening to worry about anything."

But neither of them was admiring their surroundings any longer. Their gazes fixed on each other. His brown eyes were almost black in the fading light, his stare so intense she was sure he could see past her surface to the woman she rarely showed to the world, the woman who wanted and felt so many things she couldn't find the words to express.

He leaned toward her. "Do you know what I'm thinking about right now?" he asked, his voice low.

She shook her head. "No."

"I'm remembering that kiss." He leaned closer, whispering now. "That incredible kiss."

She held her breath, willing him closer still, knowing that if he didn't kiss her again, now, she might very well shatter under the strain.

He didn't disappoint her. Their lips met and the heat of that touch melted the last of her reserve. She slipped her arms around his shoulders and held on tightly, giving herself up to the taste and feel of him. He was strong and solid and more real than any of the fears that had made her keep her distance. She'd spent the past weeks wanting nothing but this—wanting him.

His skilled mouth and caressing tongue let her know he'd wanted her, too. He pulled her onto the quilt beside him, until they pressed the full length of their bodies together.

When he finally pulled his lips away she was breathless, every part of her responding to him. He looked into her eyes and stroked his hand down her side, over her hip, a slow, languid movement that left a trail of heat along her skin. "Do you know how much I want you right this minute?" he asked.

"As much as I want you."

He kissed her again, rolling her onto her back, the weight of his body atop hers as erotic as the most intimate touch. She arched into him, pressing against his erection, frustrated by the barrier of clothing between them. She had waited so long for this moment she suddenly had no patience left.

He raised his head and looked at her once more. "What do you want to do?" he asked.

She almost laughed at the absurdity of the question. As if he didn't already know! "I want you to make love to me."

She tried to pull him down once more, but he resisted. "Not here," he said.

His words cleared away the fog of passion enough for her to remember where they were. Yes, their picnic spot was secluded, but it was still a public place, out of doors. "Come back to my place," she said.

He caressed her cheek with the back of his hand, a touch that sent a shiver of longing through her. "Are you sure?"

She nodded. "I'm sure."

He hesitated no more, but rose to his knees and turned to gather the remains of their picnic. She knelt beside him, shoving everything into the shopping bags and folding the quilt in a haphazard fashion. She felt like laughing as they hurried to the parking lot. "See you at your place," he said, leaving her with one more long, drugging kiss.

RAY STRUGGLED to stay under the speed limit as he drove behind Chrissie toward their neighborhood. When she'd told him she wanted to make love, he'd felt like shouting with relief and joy. So many things in his life had gone wrong lately; it was exhilarating to have something go right for a change.

He took deep breaths and told himself he wasn't home free yet. Chrissie might still change her mind. She'd been so skittish about him before. He wouldn't pressure her, though he'd do his best to persuade her. He could still feel her lying beneath him, arching against him, awakening all the feelings he'd denied himself for too long.

At his house, he parked in the driveway and met her in hers. Before he could say a word, she wrapped her arms around him and kissed him soundly, surprising him and delighting him with her boldness.

Smiling, she took his hand and led him inside, through the living room, down a short hall to the bedroom. "I think I like this side of you," he said.

She gave him a coy look over her shoulder. "What side is that?"

"This take-charge, knows-what-she-wants-and-intends-to-get-it woman." He pulled her close. "Not that I ever thought you were a pushover, but tonight you're showing a certain...assertiveness I find very attractive."

She slid her hands up his chest. "Oh, you do? I guess

I am feeling a little bold." She unbuttoned the top button of his shirt.

"Mmm. Don't let me stop you." He nuzzled her neck, inhaling the sweet fragrance of her skin. He kept his hands still, resting on her hips, determined to fight the urgency that pulled at him. He'd waited a long time to be with Chrissie; there was no need to rush.

She, however, had no interest in patience. She quickly had all the buttons of his shirt undone and was pushing it off his shoulders, standing on tiptoe to kiss the hollow of his collarbone. The tenderness of the gesture caught him off guard, making him feel vulnerable in a way he wasn't used to feeling, as if Chrissie was stripping away more than his clothing.

He shrugged out of the shirt, then gently pushed her back, both to allow him to begin undressing her, and for the chance to catch his breath. As he grasped the hem of the silky blouse she wore, she gave him a nervous smile. "I have to confess I'm a little nervous," she said.

He pulled the blouse up enough to stroke the smooth, soft flesh of her stomach. "That makes two of us. But hey, no one's grading our performance, right?"

The look she sent him went a long way toward burning away any jitteriness he had been feeling. "It doesn't matter," she said. "You already have an A in my book." She slipped her arms around his neck and kissed him, long and hard, stoking the fire within him to a roaring heat.

He helped her out of her sandals and skirt, then slipped off his own shoes and pants. Seeing her naked made him catch his breath. "You're beautiful," he said, caressing her hips once more.

"Mmm." She smoothed her hand over his abdomen. "You look even better than you have in my dreams."

"You've dreamed about me?" he asked, intrigued. "What kind of dreams?"

Her smile was secretive and sultry. "Erotic dreams." She grasped his hips and pulled him close. "Very erotic."

"One day you'll have to tell me more." He led her to the bed and lay down beside her, then gathered her close, determined to prove that reality could be better than any dream.

It had been a long time since Chrissie had made love to a man; she was sure it had been a while for Ray, too. But their bodies had not forgotten the moves in this most intimate of dances, and responded with the instincts of longtime lovers.

The few moments of awkwardness—when her hair was caught beneath his elbow, when they bumped heads as she shifted position—only added to the tenderness of the moment, their laughter easing some of the tension.

She couldn't get enough of looking at Ray's body, so perfectly masculine, every muscle defined. She traced the line of his broad shoulders and caressed the soft dusting of hair across his chest, then trailed her fingers across the ridges of his abdomen. "I love it when you touch me," he said, kissing her temple. "It feels so wonderful."

She thought she knew what he meant. As arousing as it was to be touched sexually, the most awful thing about living alone was the lack of simple, loving contact with another human being. She craved casual caresses, hugs and even the brief touch of a hand. She exulted now in every stroke of Ray's hand on her, whether he was caressing her bottom or breast, or merely brushing aside a lock of hair that had fallen across her cheek.

But soon simple touches were not enough. Ray had awakened a desire in her that demanded to be fulfilled. He was a skilled lover, drawing responses from her she hadn't known she had it in her to give. She was an eager partner in their lovemaking, urging him to move in a certain way, to stroke her in a particular place, or boldly touching him. Old inhibitions had been erased by need and her sheer delight in being with this man.

He didn't even hesitate when she took a condom packet from the bedside table and handed it to him. She blushed as she did so, then felt silly for doing so. The condoms had been leftover from a gag gift shower she'd thrown for Allison when she and Daniel married; at the time, Rita had jokingly stashed them in Chrissie's bedside drawer, saying maybe having them there would help her get lucky.

She'd gotten lucky all right, she thought as Ray moved over her. She opened her arms and legs to him and let out a sigh, which transformed to a satisfied moan as he entered her.

He began to stroke, slow and deep, then faster, his face transformed by his growing need. She closed her eyes and surrendered to the onslaught of sensation, feeling more alive to every touch, every vibration, than she had in years. She arched to meet him with each stroke, communicating her growing urgency as she grasped his hips.

When he reached down to stroke her, she cried out, and looked up to find him smiling down at her. The affection in that look made her eyes sting with tears. She shut her eyes again to keep him from seeing, hoping if he did he would understand these were tears of happiness.

Then all thought of tears of any kind vanished as her

body responded to him and she reached a shuddering climax that still rocked her as he also came.

She wrapped her arms around him and held him close as he emptied himself into her. When he grew still, he rolled them onto their sides and held her, unmoving, for a long while. The only sounds were their own labored breathing and the steady beating of their hearts.

I love you, Ray. She bit her lip to keep from saying the words that shouted in her head. She couldn't risk saying them first and having him react the wrong way. Instead, she pressed her cheek against his shoulder and murmured, "That was wonderful."

His arm tightened around her. "Yeah." A single syllable, little more than a grunt, but she smiled to hear it, the warmth of his hand and the strength of his hold on her telling her more than words could. Ray was a man who cared. How much, she couldn't yet say, but it was enough for now.

CHAPTER THIRTEEN

RAY LEFT CHRISSIE'S HOUSE the next morning feeling dazed. In a single night, his life had taken an unexpected, though wonderful, turn. He'd set out on their picnic intending only to remain platonic with a woman he found it easy to be with, whose friendship he valued.

But after one night in her bed he realized he'd fallen for her, and hard. He wasn't ready to use the *L* word yet, but one day soon he had no doubt it would come out.

Being in love with Chrissie felt great—and awful. Awful because he had the uneasy feeling he'd been here before. Hadn't he decided he loved Tammy after only a few dates? Hadn't he been sure the two of them were right for each other, only to be proven wrong?

He reminded himself that Chrissie was not Tammy. She was older, more mature and infinitely more sensible. And he was not the man he'd been then, either. He'd grown tougher through the years, more cynical and wary. And yet when he was with Chrissie, all those doubts evaporated.

And T.J. loved Chrissie, too, which had to be a plus. On Sunday afternoon when Ray met Tammy and their son at the family counseling center, he was relieved to see T.J. had survived his first visit with his mom well enough, though he was uncharacteristically quiet. "How was your visit with Mama?" Ray asked as he buckled his son into his booster seat.

"It was fun," T.J. said, though he didn't smile.

Further questions about what he did and what he ate drew similar unrevealing answers. Ray kept glancing in the rearview mirror at the boy, who stared out the side window of the truck, expressionless. What had happened to the boy who would spend twenty minutes telling the entire plot of a movie he saw, or describing in detail everything he'd had for lunch?

When they reached the house, Ray glanced toward Chrissie's place, but her driveway was empty. When they'd parted Saturday morning, she'd planned to spend the rest of the weekend helping her parents pack. He unbuckled T.J. and helped him out of the truck. "Are you feeling okay, sport?" he asked. "You're kind of quiet."

T.J. looked up at him for a moment, then startled Ray by bursting into tears.

Ray dropped to his knees and pulled his son close. "What's wrong?" he asked. "What happened to upset you?"

T.J.'s body shook with sobs, and Ray could hardly make out the words he was saying. "I m-miss...M-Mama!" he bawled. He wiped at his eyes with his hands and tried to sniff back the tears. "And when I was with her, I missed you. Why can't we all be together again?"

Ray didn't think it was possible to feel more rotten than he did right now. "I wish things had worked out differently," he said, pulling out a handkerchief and wiping T.J.'s face. "But your mom and I can't live together anymore. The important thing to remember is that you'll still see both of us. You'll be all right." And Ray would start saving now for a therapist, just in case.

He picked T.J. up and carried him into the house. Either the boy had gained weight at his mom's, or Ray had forgotten how big his son was getting.

"Mama said if you go back to fight in the war, I can come live with her," T.J. said when Ray set him down inside the house.

Silently cursing Tammy and her big mouth, Ray discarded the first half-dozen answers that came to mind and settled for "If I have to go back to Iraq, you'll go someplace safe. I don't know where that will be but we don't need to worry about it now. Right now you're home with me. The biggest thing you need to worry about is what you want for dinner—sloppy joes or chicken nuggets?"

The subject of food distracted the boy, at least momentarily. "Sloppy joes," he said after a moment. "And tater tots."

"Sloppy joes it is." Ray pulled a pound of ground meat from the freezer and a bag of frozen potatoes. "And Tater Tots. And green beans." He added a bag of frozen beans.

T.J. made a face. "I don't like green beans."

"But they like you. I'll make a deal with you. You only have to eat six beans."

"I don't want to eat any beans." T.J. stuck his lower lip out in a pout.

"Five beans." Ray folded his arms across his chest and fixed his son with a stern look.

T.J. folded his arms as well and continued to pout. "Three beans."

"Four, and that's my final offer."

"If I eat four beans, then you have to eat a dozillion beans."

Ray struggled not to laugh. "How many is a dozillion?"

"A lot." T.J. spread the fingers of both hands wide. "More than this many."

"That's ten fingers you're holding up. Okay, I'll eat a dozen beans. That's twelve. And you'll eat four." He doubted that counted as a real serving of vegetables, but he'd done his share of turning his nose up at vegetables as a boy, and he'd turned out all right.

The important thing was that he'd successfully distracted T.J. from the whole distressing question of where the boy would live if—he refused to think when—Ray was deployed again. It was a question Ray hoped he'd never have to answer, but experience told him he'd better come up with a plan. One that didn't include giving in to Tammy's demands, or his own inner fears.

CHRISSIE DRIFTED THROUGH WORK Monday morning with a half smile on her face, her thoughts on Ray. As she opened and sorted the weekend's mail, she remembered snatches of conversation they'd had, the dimple that formed at one side of his mouth when he smiled, and how gentle his hands had been as they caressed her. When Allison walked in and asked why she was discarding all the bills into the trash and sorting the envelopes into piles, Chrissie laughed sheepishly. "I guess I'm having a hard time getting into the Monday-morning routine," she said as she fished the correspondence out of the trash can.

"Join the club." Allison leaned against the desk. "I'm pretty distracted myself these days."

"Oh. Why is that?" Chrissie studied the receptionist. Allison looked paler than usual, and her eyes were red, as if she'd been crying. "Is something wrong?"

Allison hugged her arms across her chest. "Daniel says there's a chance his unit will be called up again soon."

Chrissy went still, the same feeling of unreality she'd had when Ray had mentioned this rumor sweeping over her. "That can't be right," she said. "He's only been home a few months."

"But if the Army decides they're needed…" Allison shook her head. "Nobody bothered to ask what I thought." Her lower lip trembled and Chrissie immediately felt terrible for her friend. Chrissie was worried about losing a man with whom she'd spent only one night—though it had been an incredible night—while Allison was facing having to say goodbye to her husband, and once more enduring the agonizing waiting and uncertainty she knew too well from Daniel's first tour of duty.

She put her arm around the receptionist and pulled her close. "I'm so sorry. I'll pray it doesn't happen. Not yet."

Rita stopped in the doorway and frowned at them. "You two look like someone took all your charge cards away," she said. "What's going on?"

Allison sniffed and said nothing, so Chrissie explained. "There's a rumor going around the base that Daniel's unit may be deployed again soon," she said.

"That's Ray's unit, too, isn't it?" Rita said.

Chrissie looked away, her expression carefully blank. "Yes, I guess it is."

"I forgot about Ray!" Allison turned to her. "How is he doing? Is his divorce final yet?"

Rita was obviously waiting for an answer, too. Chrissie gathered up all the opened envelopes and tossed them into the trash. "He's legally separated now. Tammy had T.J. for the first time this weekend."

"And did you keep the lonely single dad company?" Rita asked.

Chrissie flushed. Forget trying to keep a secret in this office. Rita and Allison had a kind of relationship radar. "We had a picnic at Garden of the Gods." *Among other things*.

"That sounds romantic." Allison dabbed at her eyes with a tissue and managed a smile. "Was it?"

"Yeah, was it?" Rita echoed.

Chrissie was saved from answering by the sound of the front door buzzer, announcing the arrival of a patient. Rita and Allison hurried up front while Chrissie retreated behind her desk, where she sat, staring at the telephone. Who could she call to confirm this nasty rumor about Ray's unit being sent back to Iraq? And what was she going to do if it was true?

She found herself dialing Ray's cell. She still had the number from when she'd kept T.J. for him. Maybe he'd heard something new this morning. And maybe hearing his voice would calm the panic building within her.

She almost hung up while she listened to the phone ringing, then he picked up. "Hi, Chrissie."

Hearing him say her name made her feel all warm and soft. "Hi, Ray," she said.

"It's nice to hear from you. I've been meaning to call, but I was busy with T.J."

The mention of the boy made her smile. "How is he?" she asked. "Did he have a good time with his mom?"

"He says he did. He had a little breakdown when we

got home. It's a lot for a little guy to adjust to." She thought he sighed. "I felt like a heel for putting him through it."

"It's not your fault," she tried to reassure him. "Sometimes things just…happen."

"Yeah, and we still have to figure out how to deal with them." She heard shuffling noises, as if he was shifting the phone to his other ear. "So how's your day going so far?" he asked.

"Okay…and not so okay. You know my receptionist, Allison? Her husband, Daniel, is in your unit."

"Yeah, I remember her. What about her?"

Chrissie took a deep breath. "She says Daniel told her there's a possibility his unit—your unit—will be deployed again soon. So maybe Tammy wasn't just making it up."

"Yeah, that's the word going around," he said. "Nothing official yet."

She slumped in the chair, feeling as if one of the lead aprons they used when X-raying patients had been draped over her. "Ray, what are you going to do?" she asked.

"I've been doing a lot of thinking," he said. "I know this might be rushing things, but after the other night…"

She held her breath, afraid of what he might say next. Matt had used much the same words when he'd proposed to her.

"I need to find a safe place for T.J. if I have to leave," he said. "And I was wondering if you'd take him."

She let out her breath in a rush and felt weak with relief and more than a little foolish. She'd expected the wrong question. But the one he had asked was almost as disturbing. "Ray, I can't take T.J. I mean, I'd love to, but I doubt the court would let him go with someone who isn't even a relative. Not when Tammy has asked to look after him."

"You're right. I just…I don't know what to do."

She sat up straight, elbows resting on the desk, relieved to have something outside herself on which to focus. "What about your parents?" she asked. "They looked after T.J. before."

"Only because Tammy caught them off guard. They made it clear they wouldn't do it again."

"But T.J. is their grandson. And if he needs them—"

"I told you, my parents aren't exactly warm people. They love T.J., in their own way. But they like being free to do their own thing."

Some people needed to be shaken, she thought. "It's not as if you're leaving voluntarily," she said. "I mean, you're serving your country."

"My dad, in particular, doesn't see it that way. He doesn't support the war."

"That doesn't mean he can't support you."

"The way they see it, they did their job raising me, I'm on my own now."

Chrissie had a hard time understanding this. No matter what happened, she knew her parents would always be there to back her. They were glad she was independent, but that didn't mean she couldn't turn to them for help, encouragement and love at all times. She'd never have come through the loss of Matt as well as she had without their support. And without them, she would truly be alone in the world. The idea was too sad to contemplate.

"You're not on your own," she said. "You have friends and you have T.J." *You have me.* She wanted to say it, but couldn't bring herself to do so. If he was leaving, she didn't really have *him.* And she needed a relationship that was a two-way street.

"Maybe you won't have to leave," she added. "Maybe it's just one of those rumors that go around and nothing comes of it."

"Yeah, maybe so," he said. "I hope so. Not just for me, but a lot of guys in my unit have barely gotten used to being back in the States. To get yanked back over there again so soon—it doesn't only hurt them, it hurts their wives and kids, everybody."

"Yeah." *It even hurts women like me, who aren't wives or even really girlfriends, but who've managed to get involved in spite of themselves.*

"I have to go now," he said. "I'll talk to you later. Want to have dinner tonight?"

"I—I can't," she said. "My mom asked me to stop by and pick up some stuff from her and I'll probably have dinner there." She hadn't planned on being at her folks' that long and could have easily made it home for dinner with Ray, but she needed to put some distance between her and him right now. Close to him, she wasn't able to think clearly.

"Talk to you soon, then," he said. "I miss you already." His voice deepened to a sexy half whisper. "It almost makes me wish T.J. was going back to his mom's sooner, just so you and I could be alone again."

She ignored the tremor of desire that tickled her gut. "You'd better go," she said. "Goodbye."

After she hung up, she stared at nothing for a long while. As much as she wished the rumor of Ray's being deployed again wasn't true, she'd lived near a military base long enough to know that almost every rumor had a grain of truth to it. If Ray's group wasn't being sent back to Iraq right away, it would be soon. There was nothing she could do to stop it. All she could do was try to limit the emotional damage Ray's leaving caused.

Maybe she was being a coward, but she never wanted to endure with Ray what she'd gone through with Matt—loving a man she scarcely knew, then losing him before anything could come of their love.

RAY HAD LONG AGO ACCEPTED that his parents were not the touchy-feely, involved-in-their-child's-life kind of mother and father many of his friends had. There were times when he wished he had a closer relationship with them, but he tried to focus on the good things they had given him, namely a sense of independence and an early reliance on his own wits to see him through any situation. He had never had to turn to anyone else for help.

Until now. Now he needed assistance not for himself, but for his son. If he didn't find someone to care for T.J. when and if he was sent back to Iraq, the boy would go by default to his mother. And Ray would spend his entire tour in knots over whether or not Tammy was going to change her mind and abandon the boy the first time she decided being a full-time mother was too boring or didn't fit into her social calendar.

Since he had no brothers or sisters or close cousins, that left his parents. They had done a good job of looking after T.J. before. The boy spoke fondly of his time with Grandma and Grandpa. They would provide a stable, safe place for T.J. to await his father's return.

The challenge would be convincing them to do the job. Ray told himself he'd faced bigger challenges before, but few for which he felt less well-equipped. Talking to his parents about a problem wasn't the same as negotiating with a Shiite warlord or an Iraqi militiaman. Blood ties and shared histories, memories of past hurts and old arguments derailed any efforts to be truly objective. And asking for help from people he secretly felt should have offered it freely felt too much like begging.

But for T.J.'s sake, he swallowed his pride and picked up the telephone. "T.J. and I want to come visit for a few days," he said when his mom answered the phone.

"Oh? When would you come?" His mother sounded more as if she was scheduling a visit with a repairman than with a beloved son and grandson.

"I was thinking this weekend. Just for a couple of nights."

"Let me see…" He heard the flipping of calendar pages. "Your father has a golf game Saturday morning, but other than that, we're free."

Heaven forbid his father cancel his regular foursome. "Great," he said. "We'll drive up Friday night. T.J.'s looking forward to seeing you."

"We'll enjoy seeing him," she said, her tone warmer now. "And you, too."

When Ray announced they were going to visit Grandma and Grandpa, T.J. looked wary. "Are we going to stay with them?" he asked.

"Just for a couple of days." Ray knelt in front of the boy, so that they were eye to eye. "I'm not going to leave you there. But if I have to go away to fight again, you might have to stay with them for a little while—just until I come home. What would you think of that?"

T.J. stuck his finger in his mouth. "I'd rather stay with you," he mumbled.

"The Army won't let me take you to Iraq," he said. "And you wouldn't like it there anyway."

"Why not?"

He debated how much to tell his son. He didn't want to frighten him, but he didn't want to lie, either. "It's dirty there, and noisy, and there's a lot of fighting," he said. "Soldiers like me are trying to make things better, but it's hard work. No fun for a kid like you. There's no television or movies or macaroni and cheese," he added.

T.J. wrinkled his nose, apparently displeased at a world without mac and cheese. "Then I'd stay with Grandma and Grandpa?" he asked.

"Right. Like you did before. Would that be okay?"

T.J. shrugged. "I guess. But I'd still rather stay with you."

"I'd rather stay with you, too." Ray patted his son's shoulder. In an ideal world he would never leave again. He would raise his son and see how this growing relationship with Chrissie developed. There was probably never a good time to go away to war, but the timing on this one couldn't be worse.

CHAPTER FOURTEEN

RAY NEVER KNEW what kind of reception he'd get from his parents, but his mom seemed happy enough to see her son and grandson when they arrived Friday evening, and she was almost cheerful as the three of them ate breakfast the next morning while Ray's dad played golf. "It looks as if you've been doing a good job of feeding him," she said as T.J. polished off the last of a stack of frozen waffles drowned in syrup. He was seated at the dining nook table while the two adults refilled their coffee mugs in the kitchen. "He must be three inches taller."

"He's an easy kid," Ray said. "You should know that."

"No child is truly easy, not even you." She lowered her voice. "What do you hear from his mother?"

"We're still working out the terms of the divorce. She has visitation rights. He spent last weekend with her."

"I suppose that's good. Though I don't really trust her."

"Yeah, well, I don't either." He took a long drink of coffee. Might as well get this over with. "There's a rumor my unit may be sent back to Iraq soon."

His mother's frown deepened. "I suppose that means T.J. will have to go with Tammy."

"Not if you and Dad will keep him."

"That's not possible." The answer was immediate, no hesitation, and she shook her head so hard her bobbed hair swung back and forth.

"Why not?" He leaned toward her. "You said yourself, Tammy isn't trustworthy. He stayed with you before and he did fine."

"Only because there was no other choice."

"I don't see that there's a choice now." She ought to realize that from the fact that he was even asking her. "If you won't take him, what's going to happen the next time Tammy decides she's tired of being a mom and runs off to her next adventure?"

She turned her back on him and began stacking dishes in the sink. "Maybe she's gotten that all out of her system now."

"Maybe. But I don't want to take a chance on that. Do you?"

She began rinsing the dishes, before loading them into the dishwasher. "Your father would never agree to it."

"Why not? T.J. is his grandson. And it's not as if I'm asking you to keep him forever—only until I return home."

She looked over her shoulder at him, her face drawn, eyes mournful. "And what if you don't come home?"

Both hands tightened around his coffee mug. "Then I'd like to think having my son here would be better than having nothing of me at all."

She looked away, but not before he saw the anguish in her eyes. "It's asking a lot," she said, scrubbing furiously at an already-clean pan.

"I know it is," Ray said. "But I wouldn't ask if I didn't believe this was the best solution for all of us."

"You'll have to talk to your father," she said, not looking up.

He was tempted to point out to her that this was a slightly more important decision than whether he could sleep over at a friend's house, but T.J.'s arrival stilled his tongue.

"Grandma, I'm finished," the boy said, holding up his empty plate and glass.

"Thank you, T.J." Ray's mother took the dishes. "Why don't you change into your swimsuit and watch cartoons until Grandpa gets home. Then I'll take you to the swimming pool while he and your father talk."

"I love swimming," T.J. shouted, and raced toward the spare bedroom he and Ray shared.

"Thanks, Mom," Ray said.

"I haven't done anything," she said. "You still have to persuade your father."

When Ray's dad returned from nine holes of golf with his regular foursome, he looked relaxed and tanned. Ray waited until he'd showered and retired to the den before he approached him.

The room was dark, the heavy draperies drawn, the television providing the only light. The screen showed images of tanks rolling into Paris. Ray stood in the doorway and stared at the incongruous scene. He might have been looking at footage of Bradley Fighting Vehicles storming Baghdad. It was an unsettling reminder of conflict in an otherwise peaceful setting.

"How was the drive?" His father surprised him by speaking first. He muted the television and glanced up at Ray from his seat in the recliner.

"Not too bad." Ray moved into the room and sat at one end of the sofa. The end closest to his dad. "The weather was good all the way and we made good time."

"Traveling at night, you missed all the construction around Lincoln. That's good."

It was the longest conversation they'd had in months. Once these observations about the drive from Colorado Springs to Omaha had been hashed out, they fell silent. People spoke of companionable silences and awkward silences—the silence between Ray and his dad was like a physical thing, a flashing neon arrow pointing to their inability to communicate anything of significance.

Ray shifted in his seat and tried to think of anything at all to cut through his father's reserve. Even disagreement was better than the polite reserve that was their norm these days. He'd come here to ask his parents for help, so maybe the thing to do was to cut to the chase. "Dad, there's something we need to talk about," he said.

"Oh?" The older man looked wary. Ray didn't blame him. Too often, their attempts at conversation disintegrated into shouting and invective, neither side listening to the other.

Ray cleared his throat, searching for the right words. The problem was, there was no right way to deliver bad news. "There's a rumor my unit may be sent back to Iraq soon," he said.

"We shouldn't be over there in the first place." The reply was automatic, exactly what Ray would have predicted.

"I know how you feel about the war," he said. "What I don't know is how you feel knowing *I'm* going to be there again."

His father looked at him, his face all pale planes and harsh shadows in the flickering artificial light. "I feel the same as I would for anyone else's son—you shouldn't be there."

Ray rested his elbows on his knees and laced his fingers together. Maybe it was stupid for him to be sitting here, trying to get through to the old man. Maybe his father really *didn't* think of him any differently than he thought of complete strangers. But how could that be?

"You know, when I look at T.J., all I can think of is how I would do anything in my power to protect him," he said. "To keep him from being hurt. He spent two nights with his mom last weekend and I worried about him almost the whole time. Does that kind of worrying stop when he gets older?"

The lines between his dad's eyes deepened. "When kids get older you trust you did a good job raising them to look after themselves."

"Is that it, then? You raised me to be my own man and if I go off and die in a conflict you don't believe in, too bad, I never should have gone?"

"I never said I wanted you to die. It's precisely because I don't that I'm opposed to this whole mess in Iraq."

"Mess or not, it's my job to go over there and to do my best—including my best to stay alive."

"You never should have joined the military in the first place. I tried to talk you out of it. You were too stubborn to listen." He focused once more on the television screen, as if there was nothing more they could have to say to one another.

"I'd say I come by my stubbornness honestly," Ray snapped. He stopped and took a deep breath. "Dad," he tried again. "I'm sorry if you feel I was disregarding your advice. The point is, I'm in the Army now and I'm probably going back to Iraq sooner rather than later. I'm not happy about it, but while I'm there, I need to focus on the job, not be distracted by what's happening here at home. I'm not asking you to support a war you don't believe in—I'm asking you to support *me*."

His father remained silent, his jaw set. Ray stifled a sigh and pressed on. "You raised me to be independent, to look after myself. I appreciate that and I've never asked you for anything since I became an adult. But I'm asking you for this. Look after T.J. for me, so I'll know he's safe."

"What does your mother say?"

"She said she'd do it if you agreed. I know this isn't how you planned to spend your retirement, but it's not as if you and Mom are old. And it's only for a little while. By taking that worry off my mind, you'll be helping me to stay safe, too."

His father stared at the television for a long moment, though Ray wondered if he was really seeing the commercial for weed killer that played. Finally, the older man nodded. "I never thought of it that way before," he said. "I never agreed with you, but I never wished you ill."

"I know that, Dad." He put his hand on the older man's shoulder. "I know that." Or at least, he'd wanted to believe it. It was good to hear his father say the words.

"We'll look after T.J. Don't you worry about that. He's a good kid." He glanced at Ray. "Reminds me of you at that age."

Ray had trouble getting the next words out, his voice gruff. "Thanks, Dad."

"Just do me a favor and don't go getting shot."

"I'll do my best." The air in the room felt lighter now, the distance between him and his father not as vast. All those hard silences had been breached by a few heartfelt words. And now he had more reason than ever to make it home safely, for T.J. and Chrissie, and for the promise of a better relationship with the people responsible for getting him here in the first place.

CHRISSIE TAPED UP yet another box of books from her parents' house and stacked it with the others in the dining room. She'd taken to stopping by a couple times a week, offering to help with the packing. But really, she wanted to enjoy a few last hours in her childhood home while she still had the chance.

"Are you still seeing that neighbor of yours?" her mother asked, following Chrissie into the dining room and adding her own box to the growing pile of cartons.

Chrissie had almost forgotten she'd mentioned Ray to her parents. "We went out again," she said, determined not to reveal too much. Her feelings for Ray were so chaotic right now; she wasn't yet ready to share them.

"That's wonderful. What did you say his name was again?"

Chrissie almost laughed at her mother's less-than-veiled attempt to get information out of her. "His name is Ray," she said. "He has a three-year-old son, T.J."

Her mother's smile was wide. "That's wonderful. I know you love children." Her mother headed back into the living room and began removing more books from the shelves. Chrissie followed. "And what does Ray do for a living?"

Chrissie sighed. Why bother concealing the truth any longer? "He's a soldier, a captain with the Sixth Cavalry."

Her mother nodded, her expression serene. "He sounds wonderful."

"He is. Except—" She trailed one hand along the edge of a row of leather-bound classics. "There's a good chance his unit is about to be sent back to Iraq."

"That makes it hard, but you can write to each other while he's away. Or e-mail or whatever the equivalent is these days." Her mother transferred a shelf of well-thumbed paperbacks to her box. "That will give you a chance to get to know each other better."

She made it sound so old-fashioned and romantic. "Mom, I don't know if I want to do that. I don't know if I can." All those months early in her marriage, when she'd written to Matt, she'd been so full of optimism and hope. This time all those good feelings would be replaced by anxiety and dread. How could she stand all those months of that kind of tension? And if something happened to Ray...

"Why not?" Her mother interrupted these thoughts.

Chrissie looked at her mother, whose face held only gentle concern. Did she really not understand? "What if I fall in love with him and something happens?" she said.

"Surely you don't think that will happen again."

"Lightning does strike twice." Chrissie hugged her arms across her chest. "We're talking about a soldier, not someone with a nice, safe job like bank teller."

"Even bank tellers can get killed in car accidents—or a robbery attempt."

"Thanks for trying to cheer me up."

Her mother sealed the box with packing tape from a

giant roll. "I'm only saying, don't let your fear keep you from living."

Chrissie didn't need her mother to remind her she was sometimes overly fearful, but where was the line between being too afraid and being sensibly cautious? If she knew she could do something to keep from being hurt again, wasn't she being smart to avoid that pain?

"Thank you for helping with the packing." Her mother picked up another empty carton and began filling it with books. "The movers are coming next Friday and there's still so much to do. We close that morning and hand over the keys to the new owner. As soon as we're settled into the new place, we'll have you to dinner. Maybe you can bring your neighbor."

"Mom!"

Her mother laughed. "You can't blame a mother for hoping." She gave Chrissie a quick hug. "I want you to be happy."

"I know." A few months ago, she would have said she *was* happy. She had work she enjoyed and a comfortable house. She had friends and close family and pets and a familiar routine. She didn't need anything else.

And then Ray had walked into the house next door and reminded her of everything that was missing in her life—a mate and companion, children of her own. Love.

She hugged a stack of books to her chest, pressing down as if she could slow the agitated pounding of her heart. Was she really in love with Ray, or only with the idea he represented? What if letting go of him was the best way for her to find the kind of man she really needed—one who wasn't in danger of leaving her and dying in a far-off war?

Tinny music sounded from across the room. "Is that your phone?" her mother asked, even as Chrissie was lunging for her purse. The caller ID showed Rita's number. Maybe her coworker wanted to get together for dinner or a movie.

"Hey, Rita," Chrissie said, grateful for the distraction from her own tortured thoughts.

"Chrissie."

The word had a leaden sound, as if spoken from deep inside a dark tunnel. Chrissie's stomach dropped somewhere near her feet and she groped for a chair. "What's happened?" she asked. "Are you all right?"

"It's Paul." More silence, followed by a heavy, wet breath. Chrissie closed her eyes and gripped the edge of the dining table so hard her knuckles ached.

"He's been wounded…IED…don't know how bad." Rita sniffed. "I'm catching a flight to Germany tonight. That's where they're taking him."

Chrissie opened her eyes again and forced herself to listen, to talk. "I'll take you to the airport. Just tell me what time. Don't worry about anything. Just tell me what to do."

Oh God, please let Paul be all right, she prayed. *Please don't let Rita have to go through what I went through.*

CHAPTER FIFTEEN

THE TUESDAY AFTER he returned from visiting his parents, Tammy called Ray and asked him to give her a hundred dollars. "Think of it as an advance on the child support you're going to owe," she said, sounding perfectly serious.

Ray gripped the phone so hard the plastic should have shattered, and considered hanging up on her, but frankly, her nerve intrigued him. "I'm the one with custody of T.J. right now," he said. "*You* should be paying *me* child support."

"I don't have any money to pay you." Her voice turned pleading. "Please, Ray. I'm really in a bind here. I know you have the money."

"I thought you had a job."

"Waitressing. It doesn't pay that much. And I had some unexpected bills this month."

"What about Kurt? He's working." Ray sometimes saw Tammy's boyfriend on base. He went out of his way to avoid the man.

"Kurt spent his money." She sounded none too pleased with her boyfriend. "Come on, Ray. For old times' sake."

He almost laughed at the absurdity of this plea. "Tammy, you left me for another man, abandoned our kid, took my furniture, stole my truck, then sold it—and now you want me to give you money because I'm feeling sentimental about our marriage? Are you crazy?"

"I didn't steal the truck. It was in my name." She sounded petulant. "If you won't give me the money for me, think of T.J. He's staying with me this weekend and I want things to be right for him."

The mention of T.J. erased all his amusement. "If you can't look after T.J., he can stay with me."

"Ray, don't be that way!" Her voice rose to an unpleasant whine. He heard the rattle of her earring against the receiver as she switched the phone to her other ear. "Look, no matter what you think, I love T.J. He means everything to me. Yeah, I screwed up, but I always—*always*—only wanted what was best for him. That's why I took him to your parents when I knew I wouldn't be able to provide a good home for him. I'd do anything for him."

"The best home for him is with me. You know that, even if you won't admit it."

"So are you and Chrissie sleeping together or what?"

This abrupt change of subject threw him off balance, as it was no doubt intended to. "Why are you even asking that question?"

"T.J. mentioned you all had dinner together a couple of times. And I could so see the two of you together. You're a lot alike—not like you and me."

"Chrissie and I are just friends." More than friends, but how much more, he wasn't sure. Now wasn't the time to explore that question too closely, with his future so uncertain.

Tammy laughed. "You just answered my question."

"What do you mean?"

"You should hear yourself. When you say her name, your voice gets this certain, I don't know, *softness*. If you're not already sleeping with her, you want to. I think you should go for it."

"So you can tell the judge I'm some tomcat who sleeps around?" he snapped.

"Hey!" She sounded offended. "I was trying to be nice. You may not believe me, but I want you to be happy. It would be great if you found someone to love. I still think you're a nice guy, even if you weren't right for me."

He blinked. Was she deliberately trying to keep him off balance, or was she serious? He'd never thought of Tammy as the devious type before. Indeed, one of the things he'd liked about her from the first was her honesty. She didn't play games or make him guess what she was feeling. If she didn't like something, she said so. She was impulsive, selfish and immature, but he seldom had to guess what she wanted or what she was feeling.

"What happens when your unit goes back to Iraq?" she asked, again shifting the conversation in a new direction.

Did she mean what would happen with Chrissie? He wished he knew. It was a subject they'd both avoided. In any case, he had no intention of discussing Chrissie any further. As far as he was concerned, the only common interest he and Tammy shared was their son.

"My parents have agreed to look after T.J.," he said. "You can still have visitation," he added.

"Your parents live in Omaha!" Her voice rose again.

"You said you'd do anything for him. There are waitressing jobs in Omaha."

She sputtered a choice obscenity and hung up on him. He closed his phone and slipped it into his pocket, thoughtful. His own detachment struck him. Even a few weeks ago he would have lashed out at Tammy, and walked around for hours nursing his rage. Now he felt nothing but mild amazement at her nerve and curiosity about her money troubles. Chrissie had mentioned that Tammy had asked her for money also.

Irresponsible as she sometimes was in other areas of her life, Tammy had never been a spendthrift. When they'd met, she'd been driving a car that was paid for and had money in the bank. During their marriage she'd handled their finances well, and had even suggested starting a college fund for T.J. shortly after he was born. Her financial responsibility was one of the reasons he hadn't hesitated to sign the truck over to her.

So why was she so broke now? The question nagged at him. He pulled out a company directory and opened his phone again, then made a call he'd told himself he wouldn't make.

"Eldridge speaking." The voice that answered the phone was that of a frog speaking through gravel. Captain Michael Eldridge was ten years older than Ray and a two-pack-a-day smoker. The two men had struck up a friendship during a training course and remained in touch.

"Mike, it's Ray."

"Ray, you old son of a gun. What are you up to?"

"I've got a favor to ask, Mike."

"Shoot. What you need?"

"You've got a soldier in your company, Private Kurt Schneider. What can you tell me about him?"

"Why do you want to know?"

"My soon-to-be ex-wife is living with him and I want to know what kind of guy my son is going to be exposed to when he visits them."

"I heard about you and your wife. Sorry about that. And I can set your mind at ease. Schneider isn't exactly a role model, but he's no child molester or druggie or anything like that. At least, not as far as I know."

"What do you know about him?"

"He's lazy. Always looking for an angle. You know the type. An officer comes around, they make like they're busy, then as soon as the uniform is out of sight, they slack off."

Ray nodded. "Any money troubles?"

"Yeah, well, I hear he likes to gamble."

"Gamble?"

"Yeah, you know, poker games, slots. He's a regular in the casinos in Cripple Creek, from what I hear. He's always mouthing off about how low his pay is, but if he'd keep his money in his wallet and stay home, he wouldn't have those kinds of problems."

"Thanks, Mike. You've helped a lot."

"Anytime. You can buy me a beer next time we see each other."

"I'll do that. Thanks."

He pocketed the phone once more. So Kurt had a gambling problem. Which meant Tammy was left to pay his bills and hers. No wonder she was broke.

Ray's lawyer would probably appreciate the information. He could use it to show that Tammy wasn't capable of supporting a child. He could even argue that the only reason she'd asked for custody was to get the child support Ray would be required to pay.

The idea made his stomach hurt. Tammy was a lot of things, but he didn't think she was that devious.

Maybe he'd ask Chrissie for her advice. Talking to her always helped him sort out his thoughts.

Which maybe proved Tammy's assertion that he and Chrissie were right for each other. He'd felt a tug in his chest when she'd said those words. In peacetime, he'd have been eager to explore the possibility further, but war complicated everything. He'd seen one marriage self-destruct in his absence. Taking a chance on a second relationship when he was about to go away seemed foolhardy.

RITA SAT beside the hospital bed in Landstuhl Regional Medical Center. Her eyes felt gritty from the tears she'd shed on the long flight to Germany, and her back ached from sitting in the hard chair, but she refused to give up her vigil. Beside her on the bed, Paul dozed fitfully, finally out of surgery, but tossing in his sleep, his hands plucking at the covers, mumbling incoherent words under his breath. His skin was sallow, a square white bandage standing out against his dark hair near his right temple, where he'd been cut by a piece of flying glass or shrapnel.

He mumbled again, and she reached over and stroked his arm, murmuring to him as she would a restless child. What was he dreaming about? Was he reliving the accident? They'd told her very little. He was on patrol, his group was engaged in a firefight. He retreated down an alley, and an IED exploded.

Her gaze shifted to the lump of bandages where his left leg had been. As much as she had stared at them, they didn't seem real. She felt numb, uncomprehending.

"Hey, you still here?"

He spoke in a raspy whisper, barely audible above the hum of monitors and the rattle of a gurney in the hallway outside the door. She took his hand in both of hers and smiled. "I don't plan to leave."

"You should get some rest."

"I will. Later." How could she sleep, knowing he was lying here, hurt? She smoothed his hair back from his forehead. He usually hated being babied, but for now he allowed it. She needed to touch him, to reassure herself that he really was here. He really was alive. "How are you feeling?" she asked.

"High as a kite. That morphine is good stuff." His smile was too brief. "How you doing? How's the peanut?"

She put her hand over her abdomen, over the barely discernible bump that was her baby. "He's fine."

Paul squeezed her hand, then slipped from her grasp and turned his head away, toward the window where thin bars of light showed through the blinds. It was late afternoon in Landstuhl, though it might as well have been the middle of the night for all Rita knew. She'd slept a little on the flight over and again in the chair she sat in now, but it wasn't nearly enough to defeat the weariness that dragged at her. She was tempted to give in to it, to close her eyes right here and now. But she hated to waste the brief time when Paul was awake and lucid.

"Your parents phoned," she said. "They were disappointed you were asleep, so they said they'd try again later."

"You should have woke me."

"I hated to. They told me rest is the best thing." She fluttered her fingers along the edge of the bed, fighting the urge to touch him again. "You lost a lot of blood."

"Yeah, that's not the only thing I lost." He lifted his head and glanced down toward the leg, deep frown lines etched between his eyebrows. "They say later I'll feel it—something called phantom pain. Right now, I don't feel anything."

"You're alive. That's all that matters to me."

"Yeah. I'm alive." He dropped his head back onto the pillow and stared at the ceiling. "Ever since it happened, I've been lying here, asking myself, why did I get hit and make it out okay, and guys like Matt and Jeremy didn't? Why did they have to die and I lived?"

The words chilled her. Was he saying he wished he'd died? "You dying wouldn't bring them back," she said.

"No, I know that. I know that now." He looked at her again, his eyes filled with surprising tenderness. "Right after Jeremy died, I was so angry," he said. "Angry at God and the world. Angry at the Iraqis. Angry at myself. He was the good son, you know? The smart one. The one who was going to set the world on fire. Everybody said it. And then he was just…gone."

She nodded. "I know."

"I didn't know how to go on without him, so I did everything to try not to think about him. It was like…I was punishing myself for being alive, for having the things he didn't have." He looked at her belly. "The baby made it worse. What was I doing bringing a new life into a world where a kid like my brother was allowed to die?"

She waited. This was the longest conversation they'd

had in months. Whether it was the morphine talking, or some burden he had to get off his chest, she didn't dare interrupt the flow of words.

He licked his dry lips. "Can I have some water?"

She held the straw to his lips and he sipped, then lay back and started talking again. "The thing is, when that IED went off, he was there."

The statement puzzled her. "Who was there?"

"Jeremy. He was there. In that alley."

She caught her breath. "What was he doing?"

He covered his eyes with the hand that didn't hold the IV. "It all happened so fast. Maybe I dreamed it all, but I don't think so. It was so real."

A tear slipped from his eye and rolled onto the pillow. Rita's own eyes stung and she swallowed hard, fighting the emotion, her whole body tensed, waiting for whatever would come next.

"We were being shot at," Paul continued. "I was looking for cover. Any cover. I ducked into that alley and there he was, just standing there. He wasn't wearing his uniform, but jeans and that old leather jacket he always wore—the one I have now in my closet at my folks' house. I froze and stared at him, scared all of a sudden. I mean, if I was seeing my dead brother, did that mean I was already dead?

"Then he ran at me and tackled me, harder than he ever could in real life. I went flying back just as the bomb went off." He took his hand away and looked at Rita again. "He saved my life. If I'd have gone all the way into that alley, it would have been a direct hit. I'd have died."

Tears streamed down her face. She made no effort to

hide them. "That sounds like something he'd do," she said. "He was crazy about you."

"I keep seeing him there, just looking at me, all sad and...like he was disappointed in me. Like I'd let him down."

"You didn't let him down." She squeezed his arm.

"But I did." He took a deep, shuddering breath, his chest rising with the effort. "After he died, I did. All that guilt and acting like such a jerk to everybody who cared about me. If he was alive, he'd have told me to cut that shit out. If there'd been time in that alley, I think that's what he'd have told me."

She leaned over and rested her cheek on his arm. "We have a lot to be thankful for," she said.

His hand came up to caress the back of her head. "Come over here a minute, will you?" he said.

She raised her head and looked at him. "Over where?"

"Get in here beside me." He patted the bed.

She glanced toward the door. "What if the nurse comes in?"

"So what? You're my wife. We're not going to get naked or anything. I just want to hold you."

She stood and folded back the covers, kicked off her shoes and crawled in beside him. His arm went around her, drawing her close. It felt so good to be close to him again this way, his body against hers. "The stump doesn't freak you out, does it?" he asked.

"No." She hadn't even noticed it until now, though she was being careful not to jar it, for fear of causing him pain.

"It freaks me out, but I guess I'll get used to it." He settled his hand around her. "They already sent a guy over to take measurements and stuff for one of those fancy computerized legs. You can even get all kinds of attachments on it, fancy paint jobs and everything." His voice trailed away, fatigue and drugs overtaking him, his eyes drifting shut, mouth going slack.

"That's great." She laid her head on his chest and closed her eyes, listening to the steady beat of his heart. "We're going to be just fine," she murmured. Now that she had Paul back, she never intended to let him go.

ON WEDNESDAY, Allison returned from lunch in tears. Chrissie took one look at her red-eyed receptionist and ushered her into an unoccupied exam room. "What's wrong?" she asked. "What happened?"

"While I was at lunch, Danny called and said they'd gotten orders today for their unit to return to Iraq. They're leaving in two weeks."

Two weeks. Chrissie sat on the edge of the exam chair, numb. "So soon."

Allison nodded. "It sucks." She grabbed a tissue from the box on the counter and blew her nose loudly.

"I'm sorry." Chrissie put her arm around the younger woman, even as her own spirits plummeted. Ray would be leaving. She'd managed to avoid seeing him since Paul's injury and Rita's flight to Germany, afraid in her fragile emotional state she'd say or do the wrong thing.

"I wasn't going to cry about this," Allison said. She sniffed and carefully dabbed at her eyes. "Military wives are supposed to be strong, right? Supporting our soldiers?"

"You're also human. It's normal to be upset."

"Danny feels terrible. I don't want to make him feel any worse." She squeezed her eyes shut. "Oh God, I missed him so much before. How am I going to do this again?"

"If you need to take some time off—"

"No." Allison shook her head. "With Rita gone you can't run this place by yourself. I'll be okay. Besides, I'll do better here than sitting around the house by myself while Danny's at the base." She tossed the wadded tissue in the trash. "I'll run to the ladies' room and freshen up and we'll get started on the afternoon patients." She flashed a wan smile. "Thanks for listening."

When she was alone, Chrissie went into her office and shut the door, where she slumped into the chair behind her desk and stared at the swirling pattern of her computer's screen saver. Every time her friends' husbands were deployed, she relived a little of her own tragedy. She saw how upset they were and remembered her own pain. And every time, she questioned why she stayed in the Springs and put herself through this.

But this time was worse. This time it felt more personal. More than anything else, this proved to her how much she'd grown to care for Ray.

Chrissie stared at the clock on the wall of her office and tried to take deep, calming breaths. She'd hardly slept last night, her mind crowded with worries for Rita and memories of the horrible days after Matt's death. *Oh God, please let Paul be okay,* she prayed for the thousandth time.

She'd expected to hear from Rita by now. The fact that she hadn't made her believe the news was bad. This was too much—too big a reminder of everything war could take away.

All these months, she'd been congratulating herself for finally getting over Matt's death, for moving on with her life.

She'd thought she was brave, inviting Ray into her life, telling herself she could handle anything life threw at her now.

And now Paul's injury was proving how wrong she'd been. Paul had been Matt's friend. Rita was her best friend. Their tragedy reminded her how fragile her supposed recovery had really been.

Proving she wasn't up to going through this again. If she didn't pull back from Ray—if she let herself fall deeper in love with him—and then something happened... She blinked back hot tears and shook her head. She couldn't do it. She wasn't that brave. Not even love was worth that kind of pain.

The phone rang and she answered it automatically. "Foley Family Dental."

"Chrissie? It's Rita."

The sound of her friend's voice sent a fresh wave of emotion washing over Chrissie. If Rita had been there with her, she would have burst into tears and thrown her arms around her friend. Instead, she struggled to pull herself together. "How are you doing?" she asked. "How is Paul?"

"I'm okay. Worn out, but okay. And Paul's okay. He's going to be fine."

Chrissie wanted to ask about his injuries, but felt she should let Rita take the lead. Instead, she asked, "Will he be coming home soon?"

"They're flying him to Walter Reed in a day or two. He'll be there for a while—a few months, I guess, under-going therapy and being fitted for a new leg."

"A new leg?" Chrissie felt cold.

"Didn't I say? I've talked to so many people—his family

and mine—I've forgotten who I've told what. He lost his left leg in the explosion. They amputated above the knee. There were some other minor injuries, but that's the biggie."

"How is he doing with that?" She tried to imagine Paul, the tough, macho Special Forces soldier, with only one leg.

"He's amazing. He actually seems okay with it. And we're talking again, like old times. He's more positive than I've seen him since Jeremy died. He's looking forward to the baby and talking about what he's going to do once his therapy is complete."

Rita's voice was so full of love Chrissie felt it through the telephone line. In spite of all that had happened, she sounded happier than she'd been in months. "It sounds like things are going to work out well for you," Chrissie said.

"They will. I know they will. I just wanted you to know what was going on."

"Thanks. We've all been worried. If you need me to do anything here—send you anything or anything like that— let me know."

"I will. I have to go now. It's late here and I need to try to get some rest."

"Tell Paul I said hello and love to you both."

"Thanks. I'll be in touch."

Allison appeared in the doorway as Chrissie hung up the phone. "The first patient is here," she said. "Do we take Arcadia Dental Insurance? It's not on the list."

Still in a daze from her conversation with Rita, Chrissie called up the appropriate file on the computer. "We take it. Guess I need to update that list. Go ahead and tell Dr. Foley his patient is here. Oh, and I just heard from Rita."

Allison's face clouded with concern. "How's she doing? How's Paul?"

"He lost his left leg in the explosion but he's going to be okay. They're sending him to Walter Reed Hospital in Washington, D.C., in a few days, where he'll have therapy and be fitted with an artificial leg."

"How awful for him."

"You'd think, but Rita says he's in really good spirits. She sounded good, too."

"She's thrilled he's still alive," Allison said. "I would be, too. I mean, I'd love Danny with one leg or no legs. I'd just be glad to have him." Her voice quavered and her bottom lip trembled. She bit it and took a deep breath. "I promised myself I wouldn't think about those things," she said. "Nothing is going to happen to him." Then she turned and hurried down the hall.

Chrissie knew the drill—don't think about the worst possibility and it wouldn't happen. She'd practiced that kind of magical thinking herself when Matt shipped out. It had helped her get through the lonely days and nights, but in some ways it had made news of his death harder to take. *This wasn't supposed to happen,* she'd screamed at the soldiers who came to deliver the news.

She no longer believed in the power of that kind of thinking, which left nothing to keep away the fear. She was relieved and grateful that Paul would be okay, but his injury proved how wrong things could go in a war zone. No one was truly safe or protected over there. And no wife or loved one was immune from hurt.

These thoughts still weighed heavily when Chrissie left the office shortly before six that evening. She was startled to see Ray's truck parked beside her car. As she approached, he got out. "Hey," he said, with a smile that made her heart beat harder and her feet move a little faster.

"Hey yourself," she said, stopping in front of him. "What brings you here?"

"I wanted to talk to you for a little bit before I pick up T.J. from day care."

All the joy his arrival had brought melted away as she took in the worried look in his eyes. "Allison told me your unit is being sent back to Iraq in two weeks," she said.

"Yeah." His shoulders sagged. "I guess there's no good time for this sort of thing, but now seems like a particularly bad time, with the custody battle and all."

And what about us? Chrissie wanted to ask, but she could only look away. "What's going to happen to T.J?" she asked.

"My parents have agreed to look after him. At least until the court says differently."

"I hope they don't hold your being deployed against you."

"Like I said, the timing sucks."

They were both silent, tension rising like heat waves between them. Then she felt Ray's hand on her arm. "It's a bad time, too, because I feel like the two of us are starting to get close," he said. "I don't want to lose that closeness."

"I don't want to lose it either." She forced herself to look at him—to really study the line of his jaw, the fullness of his lips, the jut of his nose, the fine lines beginning to form around his eyes. Every part of his face was beautiful to her and she wanted to imprint it on her mind forever.

He gathered both her hands in his. "A year is a long time, but we can write. And I'll call—"

She pulled her hand away. "No." It was the hardest word she'd ever said, and it hung in the air between them like an unexploded bomb.

Ray stared at her. "No, you won't write?"

She shook her head. "I—You're very special to me, Ray. Maybe the most special man I've met in a long time. I—I might even be in love with you. But I don't think we should make any promises with you going away."

He blinked. "You won't even write?"

She shook her head. She remembered the letters she and Matt had sent back and forth, where they'd poured out their hearts to one another. It was through those letters that she'd truly fallen in love with her new husband, the way she was sure writing to Ray would make her love for him even deeper and harder to lose.

"I don't understand." His voice had an edge of anger now. "You say you love me and you won't even write?"

She twisted her hands together, searching for the words to make him see things the way she saw them. "I'm not like you," she said. "I'm not a risk taker. You go halfway around the world and risk your life hunting terrorists. I could never do that. I've spent my whole life in this one town. I've had the same job since I graduated college. I even drive the same kind of car. The riskiest thing I ever did was marry Matt, and look how that turned out." She looked into his eyes, silently pleading for him to understand. "If I love you now, having only known you a little while, how much worse is it going to be if we spend months writing and talking on the phone? How much more am I going to worry, and how much more awful would it be if anything happened to you? I—" She swallowed a sob.

"I can't do it. I don't have it in me to go through that again."

He reached for her, as if he might gather her close, but she turned away, desperately wanting to hide her tears from him. She wrapped her arms around her stomach and willed herself to stay still, all the while so aware of the man behind her she imagined she could hear him breathing.

"I'm sorry you feel that way," he said at last, his voice rough. "I came here today to tell you that I love you. Those are words I thought I might never say again, after the way Tammy hurt me. But now I see they're wasted on you."

A car door slammed, an engine raced, then his truck roared out of the parking lot, tires squealing as he sped onto the highway.

Chrissie stood there a long while, hunched over, silently crying. She told herself it was better to end it between them now, in the early days, that if it was hard on them now, it would be unbearable later.

But none of these rationalizations eased her grief. She believed she was doing the only thing she could do, but she couldn't shake the feeling that she'd thrown away something precious. Something she could never get back.

CHAPTER SIXTEEN

RAY'S EMOTIONS following his talk with Chrissie rico-cheted between hurt and anger. What was all that talk about fear and courage when he was the one going off to fight? He had counted on her to be the one strong anchor in his chaotic life and she'd let him down. Chrissie—the one person he'd thought would never let him down. Was he such a poor judge of people that he'd mistaken her feelings for love? Or was it only that he'd let his own love for her color all his perceptions?

The result was the same. He was alone again, headed off into an uncertain future. He felt empty inside. He wanted to scream or punch something, but he could do none of these things because he had to pick up T.J. He tried not to let his son see how upset he was, but the boy was so quiet on the ride home, Ray wondered if he sensed some of his father's inner turmoil.

When they reached the house, Ray was surprised to see a familiar battered blue car parked at the curb. "That's Mama's car," T.J. said.

Ray groaned. Had Tammy come to beg for money in person? He helped T.J. out of his car seat, then followed the boy up to the house, where Tammy waited by the front door. "I'm not in the mood to deal with any of your games today," Ray said before she opened her mouth.

She ignored him and knelt to gather T.J. into her arms. "How was school today?" she asked him, smiling.

"It was good. We drew pictures and at recess we played a new game…." For the next two minutes she listened patiently as T.J. recited his day's activities. She nodded and made appropriate comments, then hugged the boy again. "Your dad and I need to talk for a minute," she said. "Why don't you go inside and put your things in your room?"

T.J. looked up at Ray. "Can I have a snack?"

"There are carrot sticks and dip in the refrigerator," Ray said. "You can have those, but don't make a mess."

"Okay." He flew into the house, a whirl of energy and excitement who left a void in his absence.

Ray turned to Tammy once more. "If you're here to ask for money, the answer is still no."

"I'm not here to ask you for anything," she said. "In fact, I'm going to give you something."

He frowned. "What are you going to give me?"

She folded her arms across her stomach and began to pace back and forth across the narrow front porch. "I've been thinking about what you said, about me not being able to look after T.J. and needing to get my house in order and everything."

This was an argument he wanted to stop before it started. No matter what she said, she was never going to persuade him T.J. would be better off with her. "I know about Kurt's gambling problem," he said.

She spun around and fixed him with a hard gaze. "Don't sound so superior," she said. "Yes, Kurt has a problem with gambling, but he's working on improving and I love him in spite of it. You can't imagine that, can you—loving someone in spite of their flaws? Loving them even when they don't live up to your ideal?"

Her words were like blows, taunting him. What had he done to deserve them? "What are you talking about?"

"I'm talking about accepting people for who they are, weaknesses and everything, and loving them anyway," she said. "We never had that."

"I loved you," he said, anger flaring. "God knows why, but I did."

"You loved your *idea* of me. You were so caught up in the whole 'happy home and family' thing you never even saw the real me. I tried to tell you I wasn't ready to settle down but you wouldn't listen. You kept after me so long I started to believe I could be the woman you wanted. And then you left and I felt trapped in a life that wasn't right for me."

"And Kurt is right for you?"

"Yes! Because Kurt loves me—not what I could be or what I ought to be, but *me*. Yeah, he has problems, but he doesn't expect me to fix them."

Ray wanted to argue that she was wrong, but the truth in her words cut through any denials he might have made. For an instant, he saw himself through her eyes—a man desperate not to be alone, to have the close family he'd been denied as a child. When Tammy had gotten pregnant, he'd seen his chance. But he'd never really taken her feelings into account. He bowed his head. "I never knew you felt this way," he said.

"I know I hurt you when I left," she said, her voice

softer now. She moved closer to him. "And I'll never forgive myself for hurting T.J. I thought I was doing what was best for him, that as a little kid it wouldn't matter so much to him. If I could go back and do things differently, I would, but I can't." She bowed her head and fumbled in her purse, tears dripping onto her hands.

Ray fished a handkerchief from his pocket and handed it to her.

"Thanks," she said, and blew her nose loudly.

"Why did you come here this afternoon?" he asked.

She sniffed. "I'm dropping my bid for custody."

Ray thought he might have stopped breathing for a minute. "You are?" he asked when he found his voice again.

She nodded and wadded the handkerchief in her fist. "I want to be able to look after T.J.—to try to make up for leaving him before. But maybe now isn't the right time. Kurt needs to get this gambling thing worked out and things need to be more stable before I bring a kid into the mix." She made a face. "I guess you're not the only one trying to make a situation into something it's not. I want to be the perfect mother to my son, but I'm not there yet."

"So you're saying I can have custody?"

She nodded. "As long as I still get to see him and be his mom."

The strength of the relief, joy and sadness that flooded him at this news staggered Ray. He took a deep breath and cleared his throat. "You'll always be his mother. He's crazy about you."

She nodded and wiped away fresh tears. "I know. He's a great kid. I'm glad you talked me out of having an abortion. That's one thing you definitely did right."

He laughed. "I'm glad there was something." Then he sobered. "The official orders came down today. I'm going back to Iraq."

She nodded. "That was another reason I came this afternoon. So I guess T.J. will be going to your parents in Omaha?"

"Yes. What will you do?"

"I already told Kurt I have to go there. I've got a girl-friend there who said I can stay with her. I'll find a job and get an apartment. Kurt's discharge should come through in January, so he can join me then. In the meantime, he's promised to work on the gambling thing."

"You're not worried he'll find someone else if you leave?"

Her eyes met his, clear and shining with a certainty that took his breath away. "I know you don't believe me, but our love is stronger than that. It's the reason I was willing to risk everything. Kurt and I are going to stay together, I'm sure of it."

Ray had never been so sure of anything, but he didn't say so. Tammy had given him a real gift this evening in dropping her petition for custody. He would do nothing to ruin the moment. "Thanks," he said instead. "You're doing the right thing and I appreciate it."

She nodded. "It wasn't easy for me to come here today, but I wanted things right between us before you left." She glanced toward the house. "Can I see T.J. again before I go?"

That she was asking his permission touched him deeply. "Of course. If you want, you can stay for dinner. He'd like that."

Her smile reminded him for a moment of the girl who

had first enchanted him so. "I'd like that, too. Just let me call Kurt and let him know where I'll be."

He followed her inside, marveling at the turn life had taken. If only Chrissie were here with them, everything would be perfect.

But, as Tammy had pointed out, he couldn't make a perfect life merely by wishing it so. Chrissie wasn't going to love him just because he wanted her to.

CHRISSIE MOURNED HER PARTING from Ray the way she'd grieved for every one of her life's big changes, from her cat running away when she was seven to leaving the apartment where she and Matt had spent their brief married life. It didn't matter that some of those changes—like moving out of the apartment and saying goodbye to Ray—were necessary and for the best. She left little pieces of herself behind with every parting.

Ray had taken a larger piece than most. Nights when she lay in bed, she wondered if she would ever be whole again without him.

Then she reminded herself that if letting go of him now was this bad, how much worse it would have been once they were truly entrenched in each other's lives?

So she went through the motions of each day, avoiding looking over at the house next door, timing her arrivals and departures so she wouldn't run into him, and turning her attention to other things.

Allison was preparing for Danny's departure, determined to keep a cheerful outlook, to make things as easy as possible for him. "He knows I'm going to miss him, and that it will be hard," she told Chrissie as they readied for another day of patients at the dentist's office. "But talking about it doesn't make things any better. I'd rather focus on making the time he has left here at home the best it can be."

"If you need a shoulder to cry on once he's gone, you know I'm here," Chrissie said.

Allison nodded. "I'm already making plans for things I can do to help myself stay strong while he's away," she said. "I've signed up for a yoga class. That's supposed to help a lot with stress and anxiety. And I'm going to be part of a support group that's forming at the base for the wives of men who are deployed. We can get together and share our problems and help each other out."

"That's a great idea," Chrissie said. "I had no idea there even was such a thing."

"As the war drags on, people are figuring out there's a need for this kind of thing. There are even groups for the kids. It's supposed to be a big help. And that way, nobody feels so alone, you know?"

Chrissie nodded, marveling at the younger woman's optimism and strength.

A week before the soldiers were supposed to ship out, Rita dropped by the office, surprising them all. Even Dr. Foley set aside his drill and probes to come up front and give her a hug. "I'm only in town for a few days to close up the apartment," she explained. "I'm moving into family quarters near Walter Reed, to be close to Paul while he completes his rehabilitation."

"How is he doing?" Allison asked, anxiety pinching her face.

"He has good days and bad days. He gets frustrated

sometimes, and some days the pain is bad. But he's going to be okay."

"That's good," Allison said. "We're all glad of that."

The phone rang and Allison went to answer it, and Dr. Foley returned to his patient, leaving Rita and Chrissie alone. "How are you holding up, really?" Chrissie asked.

"I'm doing good." Rita put her arm around her friend. "I know it sounds crazy, but a lot of good has come out of this. Paul is more himself than he was after Jeremy's funeral. It's as if this close call has made him see what's really important in life." She rubbed her hand across her expanding abdomen. "He's so excited about the baby. He talks to him all the time and has all these plans for him."

"What if it's a girl?"

Rita laughed. "Then it will probably be worse. He probably won't let her out of his sight until she's thirty."

"What's he going to do once he's discharged?"

"He's talking about going to college and studying to become a teacher. He wants to teach on the reservation."

"Would you like that, living on the reservation again?"

"There was a time I couldn't wait to get away from the place, but now…" She shrugged. "They need teachers there. They could probably use a dental hygienist, too. I think it doesn't matter so much where we live, as long as we're together."

Chrissie felt a tightness in her chest at these words. Oh, to have that kind of strength and resilience. She had a hard time imagining it.

"I have to go now," Rita said. "I just wanted to stop by and say goodbye to everyone."

"I don't want you to leave," Chrissie said.

Rita hugged her. "We'll stay in touch. And if you're ever in South Dakota, I expect a visit."

"Absolutely." Chrissie smiled and blinked back tears, but felt the pain of one more loss.

That evening, she was especially restless. No book or television show could hold her interest. She paced, her agitation frightening the cats. Sapphire hid under the bed and Rudy retreated to the top of a bookshelf, where he eyed her balefully.

She looked out her kitchen window, at the lights burning in Ray's house. What was he doing over there? Was he packing, or reading to T.J.? How was he preparing his son for his departure?

Was he thinking of her at all? She felt suddenly foolish, standing here with her heart so full of love, only fear keeping her from acting on her feelings. Why was she so afraid when all around her others were being brave and reaping the rewards?

Paul's accident had made the possibility of some harm falling on Ray seem all too real. Yet Rita talked of all the good that had come from that tragedy, and how it had made her and Paul close again.

Even Allison, young as she was, had a healthier attitude about supporting her man and herself than Chrissie did. Instead of sitting at home brooding and worrying, Allison planned to take classes and be a part of a support group, focusing on staying positive.

Why couldn't Chrissie do the same thing? She would probably have bad days, but maybe if she chose to think more of the good things than the bad she'd get through the rough times until she and Ray could be together again. And odds were they would be together. Dwelling on any other possibility accomplished nothing and only spoiled today. The question remained: was it too late to ask Ray to try again? Or had she ruined everything already?

As she turned from the window, she heard Ray's truck in the driveway. Quickly, before she could change her mind, she rushed out the door and met him at the side of his driveway.

"Hello, Chrissie." He nodded to her, his expression guarded. "Did you need something?"

You, she wanted to shout. But she wasn't ready yet to make that declaration. Not until she knew his own feelings. Better to begin with a less emotionally charged topic of conversation. She glanced into the truck. "Where's T.J?"

"Tammy took him for the afternoon. She wants to spend some extra time with him before he leaves for Omaha to stay with my parents."

"It's nice that you're letting her do that."

"Yeah, well, she dropped her request for custody. And she's moving to Omaha so she can be there for T.J. while I'm away."

"That's great." She couldn't bear to look at his stern face anymore, so she focused her attention on the gleaming hood of the truck. "I guess you're getting everything ready to leave," she said.

He was quiet for a long moment. She imagined she could feel his gaze on her. Was he wondering what he ever saw in her? Or thinking how he might hurt her the way she'd hurt him? Or regretting that things hadn't worked out between them? "Almost everything," he said.

Her courage was fading fast. She had to hurry. "Ray, I—I owe you an apology," she blurted.

She looked up, hoping to find some encouragement on his face. "For what?" he asked.

"For saying I wouldn't write to you." She found some last reserve of courage and made her voice stronger. "I do love you, and I want our love to be stronger than my fear."

He said nothing for a long moment, his gaze fixed on her, his mouth a hard line. She feared she'd waited too late, but then he spoke, his voice rough with emotion. "I owe you an apology, too," he said.

She widened her eyes, startled by this admission. "Whatever for?"

He shoved his hands in his pockets. "Tammy and I had a long talk. She made me see some things I hadn't realized before. I went into my relationship with her thinking only about what I wanted, thinking mine was the only opinion that mattered. I had this idea that if I married her and had a family—if I had someone waiting for me to come home, some anchor to a life outside the war zone—then somehow that would help me make it back all right." His expression grew more sorrowful. "I wanted that so much I didn't even see what she wanted. I'm afraid I looked at you a lot the same way. I loved you as much for what I wanted you to be as for what you are."

"And what do you think of me now?" she asked.

"I'd like to set aside all those notions about what I want and let you give me whatever you can. I have an idea the real thing is better than any fantasy I could come up with."

"Oh, Ray." They came together in a fierce kiss, an embrace full of longing and regret and hope and passion that made her feel like flying or shouting—or like dragging him into her house and not letting him out of her bed for days.

When their lips parted at last, he looked down on her, his eyes filled with tenderness. "I don't blame you for being afraid," he said. "You think this doesn't scare me, too? I get the shakes when I remember how I've already screwed up one marriage. And that didn't hurt only me—it hurt my son, too. The idea that I might screw up his life again, never mind my own, scares me spitless."

He stroked his knuckles along one cheek. "But when I get scared, I look at you and know the feelings we have for each other aren't a mistake. We've both been through the fire and we've got some scars, but it's made us wiser. The kind of love we have is wiser and that's nothing to be afraid of."

"But I am afraid," she whispered.

"Yeah. Me, too." He wrapped both arms around her waist and pulled her tightly against him. "When I married Tammy, I thought that love could keep me safe. It may not be able to keep me safe, but it can remind me of everything I have to live for. I promise I'll do my damnedest to come home to you and to T.J."

"Every day you can remember that my love and prayers go with you," she said. "That may not make you invincible, but it could help. You never know."

He smiled. "You know the definition of courage, don't you?" he asked.

"What's that?"

"It's being afraid and doing what you have to do in spite of that fear. We can be braver together than we ever could be apart."

"Yes." She closed her eyes and welcomed another kiss.

She made a silent pledge to be grateful for every moment they had together, to not let worries about bad things that might happen steal anything from the good times. To love him always, in spite of her fear.

EPILOGUE

"HERE COMES THE BRIDE, all dressed in white!" T.J. laughed and darted away as Chrissie pretended to lunge toward him. Almost five years old, he was getting tall, and losing more of his toddler chubbiness.

"Just be glad he's not singing the version I learned at his age." Ray, handsome in his dress uniform, winked at her and began to sing in a rusty baritone. "Here comes the bride, big, fat and wide."

"Oh, you." She slapped at him playfully, though nothing he could have said or sung would spoil this wonderful moment. She held up her left hand and for the twentieth time since the ceremony half an hour before, admired the white-gold-and-diamond wedding set residing on her third finger. After seventeen months, one hundred and fifty-six long-distance telephone conversations, over one thousand e-mails and seventy-two handwritten letters—all of which she'd saved, along with the printed-out e-mails—she was now officially Mrs. Ray Hughes.

"When is it my turn to kiss the bride?" Paul Red Horse, resplendent in a Western-style suit with a turquoise-and-silver string tie, his now-long hair worn in a single braid down his back, leaned in to buss her cheek.

Beside him, Rita adjusted their fourteen-month-old daughter, Hannah, on her hip. "Who wants to hold Hannah while Paul and I dance?" she asked.

"I will!" Allison held out both arms, and gathered Hannah to her, the little girl's legs straddling Allison's hugely pregnant belly. "I need the practice," she said, nuzzling Hannah's cheek.

"Maybe you should sit down." Allison's husband, Danny, frowned at her. "You don't want to go into labor right here."

"I'm not due for a good three weeks yet," Allison said. "Relax."

"Right." If anything, Danny looked more uptight.

"Don't worry, my man," Paul said, slapping Danny on the back. "One thing you'll figure out is that, in the early days at least, Mom does most of the work. Your job is to fetch and carry and to practice saying 'yes, dear.'"

He dodged a mock blow from Rita, then led her onto the dance floor. Ray turned to Chrissie. "Mrs. Hughes, would you like to dance?"

"I'd love to, Mr. Hughes."

As they swayed to an up-tempo rendition of "I Hope You Dance," Ray smiled down at her. "How long before we can blow this joint and start the honeymoon?"

"We should stay a little longer," she said. "When is Tammy picking up T.J.?"

"She and Kurt are supposed to be here at seven-thirty."

"Then you've got ten minutes."

"She'll be here. She's counting on us returning the favor when she and Kurt tie the knot next month."

"I'm glad they're doing well," she said, laying her head on his shoulder.

He gathered her closer. "Me, too. It makes it easier for T.J. Easier for all of us."

The months while Ray had been in Iraq certainly hadn't been easy, but Chrissie had learned so much in that time—about her husband-to-be, and about herself. Most of all she had learned that some gambles paid off in ways she'd never imagined. She'd thought of herself as a coward before, but Ray had helped her discover her own courage. She had so much to be thankful for now, all because she'd risked everything and opened up her heart and invited love in.

Love Inspired
HISTORICAL

*Powerful, engaging stories of romance,
adventure and faith set in the past—
when life was simpler and faith played a
major role in everyday lives.*

See below for a sneak preview of
HIGH COUNTRY BRIDE
by Jillian Hart

*Love Inspired Historical—
love and faith throughout the ages*

Silence remained between them, and she felt the rake of his gaze, taking her in from the top of her wind-blown hair where escaped tendrils snapped in the wind to the toe of her scuffed, patched shoes. She watched him fist up his big, work-roughened hands and expected the worst.

"You never told me, Miz Nelson. Where are you going to go?" His tone was flat, his jaw tensed as if he were still fighting his temper. His blue gaze shot past her to watch the children going about their picking up.

"I don't know." Her throat went dry. Her tongue felt thick as she answered. "When I find employment, I could wire a payment to you. Rent. Y-you aren't think-ing of bringing the sher-rif in?"

"You think I want *payment?*" He boomed like winter thunder. *"You think I want rent money?"*

"Frankly, I don't know what you want."

"I'll tell you what I don't want. I don't want—" His words cannoned in the silence as he paused, and a passing pair of geese overhead honked in flat-noted tones. He grimaced, and it was impossible to know what he would say or do.

She trembled, not from fear of him, she truly didn't

believe he would strike her, but from the unknown. Of being forced to take the frightening step off the only safe spot she'd known since she'd lost Pa's house.

When you were homeless, everything seemed so fragile, so easily off balance, for it was a big, unkind world for a woman alone with her children. She had no one to protect her. No one to care. The truth was, she'd never had those things in her husband. How could she expect them from any stranger? Especially this man she hardly knew, who was harsh and cold and hardhearted.

And, worse, what if he brought in the law?

"You can't keep living out of a wagon," he said, still angry, the cords still straining in his neck. "Animals have enough sense to keep their young cared for and safe."

Yes, it was as she'd thought. He intended to be as cruel about this as he could be. She spun on her heel, pulling up all her defenses, and was determined to let his upcoming hurtful words roll off her like rainwater on an oiled tarp. She grabbed the towel the children had neatly folded and tossed it into the laundry box in the back of the wagon.

"Miz Nelson. I'm talking to you."

"Yes, I know. If you expect me to stand there while you tongue-lash me, you're mistaken. I have packing to get to." Her fingers were clumsy as she hefted the bucket of water she'd brought for washing—she wouldn't need that now—and heaved.

His hand clasped on the handle beside hers, and she could feel the life and power of him vibrate along the thin metal. "Give it to me."

Her fingers let go. She felt stunned as he walked away,

easily carrying the bucket that had been so heavy to her, and quietly, methodically, put out the small cooking fire. He did not seem as ominous or as intimidating— somehow—as he stood in the shadows, bent to his task, although she couldn't say why that was. Perhaps it was because he wasn't acting the way she was used to men acting. She was quite used to doing all the work.

Jamie scurried over, juggling his wooden horses, to watch. Daisy hung back, eyes wide and still, taking in the mysterious goings-on.

He is different when he's near to them, she realized. He didn't seem harsh, and there was no hint of anger—or, come to think of it, any other emotion—as he shook out the empty bucket, nodded once to the children and then retraced his path to her.

"Let me guess." He dropped the bucket onto the tailgate, and his anger appeared to be back. Cords strained in his neck and jaw as he growled at her. "If you leave here, you don't know where you're going and you have no money to get there with?"

She nodded. "Yes, sir."

"Then get you and your kids into the wagon. I'll hitch up your horses for you." His eyes were cold and yet they were not unfeeling as he fastened his gaze on hers. "I have an empty shanty out back of my house that no one's living in. You can stay there for the night."

"What?" She stumbled back, and the solid wood of the tailgate bit into the small of her back. "But—"

"There will be no argument," he bit out, interrupting her. "None at all. I buried a wife and son years ago, what was most precious to me, and to see you and them neglected like this—with no one to care—" His jaw ground again and his eyes were no longer cold.

Joanna didn't think she'd ever seen anything sadder than Aiden McKaslin as the sun went down on him.

* * * * *

Don't miss this deeply moving story
HIGH COUNTRY BRIDE
Available July 2008
From the new
Love Inspired Historical
line

Also look for
SEASIDE CINDERELLA
by Anna Schmidt
Where a poor servant girl and a
wealthy merchant prince
might somehow make a life together

REQUEST YOUR FREE BOOKS!
2 FREE NOVELS PLUS 2 FREE GIFTS!

HARLEQUIN®
Super Romance®

Exciting, emotional, unexpected!

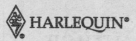

Lawyer Audrey Lincoln has sworn off
love, throwing herself into her work
instead. When she meets a much younger
cop named Ryan Mercedes, all her logic
is tossed out the window, and Ryan is
determined that he will not let the issue
of age come between them. It is not until
a tragic case involving an innocent child
threatens to tear them apart that Ryan
and Audrey must fight for a way to
finally be together....

Look for

TRUSTING RYAN
by Tara Taylor Quinn

*Available July
wherever you buy books.*

SAVE $1.00

A riveting trilogy from
BRENDA NOVAK

- -

SAVE $1.00

on the purchase price of one book in The Last Stand trilogy from Brenda Novak.

Offer valid from May 27, 2008, to August 30, 2008.
Redeemable at participating retail outlets. Limit one coupon per purchase.

52608328

5 65373 00076 2 (8100) 0 11499

Thoroughbred Legacy

The purse is set and the stakes are high...

Romance, scandal and glamour set in the exhilarating world of horse racing!

Follow the 12-book continuity, starting in July with:

Flirting with Trouble, **Book #1**
by *New York Times* **bestselling author**
ELIZABETH BEVARLY

Biding Her Time, **Book #2**
by **WENDY WARREN**

Picture of Perfection, **Book #3**
by **KRISTIN GABRIEL**

Something To Talk About, **Book #4**
by **JOANNE ROCK**

*Available wherever books are sold,
including most bookstores, supermarkets,
discount stores and drugstores.*

COMING NEXT MONTH

#1500 TRUSTING RYAN • Tara Taylor Quinn
For Detective Ryan Mercedes, right and wrong are clear. And what he feels for
guardian ad litem Audrey Lincoln is very right. Their shared pursuit of justice
proves they're on the same side. But when a case divides them, can he see
things her way?

#1501 A MARRIAGE BETWEEN FRIENDS • Melinda Curtis
Marriage of Inconvenience
They were friends who married when Jill needed a father for her unborn child,
and Vince offered his name. Then, unexpectedly, Jill walked out. Now, eleven
years later, Vince Patrizio is back to reclaim his wife…and the son who should
have been theirs.

#1502 HIS SON'S TEACHER • Kay Stockham
The Tulanes of Tennessee
Nick Tulane has never fallen for a teacher. A former dropout, he doesn't go
for the academic type. Until he meets Jennifer Rose, that is. While she's busy
helping his son catch up at school, Nick starts wishing for some private study
time with the tutor.

#1503 THE CHILD COMES FIRST • Elizabeth Ashtree
Star defense attorney Simon Montgomery is called upon to defend a girl who
claims to be wrongly accused of murder. Her social worker Jayda Kavanagh
believes she's innocent. But as Simon and Jayda grow close trying to save
the child, Jayda's own youthful trauma could stand between her and the love
Simon offers.

#1504 NOBODY'S HERO • Carrie Alexander
Count on a Cop
Massachusetts state police officer Sean Rafferty has sworn off ever playing
hero again. All he wants is to be left alone to recover. Which is perfect,
because Connie Bradford doesn't need a hero in her life. Unfortunately, her
grieving daughter does…

#1505 THE WAY HOME • Jean Brashear
Everlasting Love
They'd been everything to each other. But Bella Parker—stricken with
amnesia far from home—can't remember any of it…not even the betrayal
that made her leave. Now James Parker has to decide how much of their past
he should tell her. Because the one piece that could jog her memory might
destroy them forever.

HSRCNM0608